CANADIAN

DREADFUL

AN ANTHOLOGY

Edited by
David Tocher

Canadian Dreadful

Copyright © 2019

ISBN: 978-1-928104-15-5
eISBN: 978-1-928104-16-2

Cover Art © by François Vaillancourt
www.francoisvaillancourt.com

Cover Design © by Evan Dales
WAV Design Studios
www.wavstudios.ca

.

Dark Dragon Publishing
88 Charleswood Drive
Toronto, Ontario
M3H 1X6
CANADA
www.darkdragonpublishing.com

Printed in the United States of America.

Contents

FORWARD
    Karen Dales i
INTRODUCTION
    David Tocher iii
ARANZAZU BANKS
    Robin Rowland 1
CENTRE ICE
    Cailtin Marceau 22
HIS COLD COFFIN
    Tyner Gillies 30
MEMORIES OF MISS MINDY TULANE
    Jen Frankel 48
NOWHERE TIME
    Pat Flewwelling...61
REBECCA RAVEN
    David Tocher...72
RELENTLESS
    Repo Kempt...89
SINS OF THE FATHER
    Colleen Anderson.......................................105
SNOW ANGEL
    Nancy Kilpatrick..118
THE DELIVERY BOY
    Judith Baron...128
THE MANSION
    Karen Dales 140
TWO TREES
    Vanessa C. Hawkins....................................148
STAG AND STORM
    Sara C. Walker 160
THE SOUND OF PASSING TRAFFIC
    Joe Powers 174
BIOGRAPHIES 185

Canadian Dreadful

Dreadful

AN ANTHOLOGY

Edited by
David Tocher

Dark Dragon Publishing
Toronto, Ontario, Canada

This anthology is dedicated to the memory of Carmen Marie Hudson.

You still brighten the room and you're still the life of the party.

Forward

An anthology is a daunting task. It is no wonder that many publishers choose not to undertake this awesome responsibility. Dark Dragon Publishing has always produced spectacular novel length works by amazing authors, so this anthology is a new venture.

For years, DDP has contemplated putting together an anthology, but what theme would we want that had not been done before? How can we make an anthology unique? When David Tocher approached us with his idea, we realised that our patience, and in part our indecision, paved the way for the Universe to send a Dragon with a vision we could not grasp until he delivered it to us.

At first, we were unsure about whether we could take on this project, but with some serious soul searching and talking with David, we knew we had to publish it. Finding the writers took time and patience, and David did a spectacular job in accepting the stories that fit the vision he held. Then came the task of editing all the manuscripts to make them shine, which is akin to juggling with a dozen or more balls, each author with their own unique voices to buff and polish.

This anthology is unique in so many ways. Its title sheds some dark light onto what to expect, but it is the stories that are distinctly Canadian, written by Canadian authors, many who have been published before, some who are new. Every place that these stories bring to life will take you from one end of our great country to the other—from the Atlantic coast to the Pacific and even to the Arctic. That in itself makes this anthology special, but its uniqueness is that there is an historic or mythological element. There is a kernel of truth in every story.

Some may recognise the places in which these stories occur. Many will not. But in all cases, if you find yourself wandering Canada's many rich landscapes and waterways, you may discover that you have slipped into the realm of the Canadian Dreadful.

One in which we hope you will enjoy.

Karen Dales
June 2019

Introduction

Horror and the Heart

Those of us who are fans of horror have loved the genre since early childhood. We were born with an affection for the werewolf's howl and mist-shrouded graveyards at night.

Misled, yet well-meaning adults told us we would grow out of it. But we didn't, did we? Because horror fiction is like an oversized hand-me-down sweater. You don't grow out of it; you grow *into* it.

For instance, when I read *The Shining* at eleven years old, one scene frightened me so badly that I threw the book across my bedroom. I reread the novel twenty-four years later and this time I understood the nuanced commentary on addiction, fighting inner demons, isolation, and struggling to be a good parent.

To write horror, you must find that balance between your adult understanding of the world and your childish desire to jump out of a closet in the dark and yell "Boo!" at a terrified friend.

I believe that all fourteen authors in Canadian Dreadful

accomplish just that. Every author has something important to say about life—whether it be about grief, addiction, ending negative family patterns, betrayal, heartbreak, or survival. But they also give you what you came for:

The scares.

In these pages, you won't find the Canada you're accustomed to, nor will you find a caricaturized version where Bob and Doug McKenzie sing *"roo coo coo coo roo coo coo..."* as you order your double-double at Timmies and go for a rip. No. In our version of Canada, you'll find a landscape filled with cannibalism, human sacrifice, lonesome walks through purgatory, unrestful ghosts, mystical forest creatures, and yes, even talking mandrakes. This is **Canadian Dreadful**.

Do yourself a favour and read all the stories—not just that one by the author you're friends with (yeah, I called you out, didn't I?). There are names in here you'll recognize and some you won't. Don't play it safe and stick with the familiar. Venture into the unknown. Discover new voices in Canadian horror fiction. Remember that an anthology is like an oversized hand-me-down sweater. At first, it's a few sizes too big for you. But as you keep reading, you grow into it.

David Tocher
June 2019

Aranzazu Banks

By Robin Rowland

ll stations. All stations. This is Prince Rupert Coast Guard Radio. Prince Rupert Coast Guard Radio. At one zero three three hours, this day, this station received a report of an overdue vessel. It is a two eight foot aluminum fishing boat, make unknown, silver and green in colour, with the name *Ogygia* on the stern. Oscar Golf Yankee Golf India Alpha with one person and one cat on board. This vessel left Barnard Harbour at about one one one four hours on two five May bound for Queen Charlotte City. The *Ogygia* has now been reported to be five days overdue for arrival. Any vessels or stations with knowledge of the *Ogygia* or knowing its whereabouts please contact this station. If you spot this vessel, please have it contact Prince Rupert Coast Guard Radio and report condition. Prince Rupert Coast Guard Radio out.

May 24 16:45

Arrived at Barnard Harbour after a great day on Whale Channel. Caught a halibut and watched the humpbacks. Got

Aranzazu Banks

some great video and stills. Thought I spotted a fin whale but not sure. Surprise! Have the docks all to myself, except, of course, a couple of hundred seagulls. Lir, as can be expected of a ship's cat, hisses and lunges if the gulls get too close to his (not my) territory. I'm keeping the halibut on ice, so cousin Jake and I can eat it once I get to Haida Gwaii. The bioluminescence seems particularly active today. Saw a bit of a trail of turquoise from a couple of the swimming Stellar sea lions I passed on the way in. After I save this, I'll pee over the side to see the dancing blue light. Dinner tonight, prawn mac and cheese. By myself. Why can't I have a shipmate? Barnard Harbour at sunset is so beautiful, it's a shame I have no one to share the view.

21:34

Prawn mac and cheese was great if I do say so myself. After, walked up and down the dock with Lir, so we both could stretch our legs. The biolum is the best I've ever seen. Took another pee into the ocean after dinner. Usually, it's a bit of blue and green that dances around the pee bubbles and then fades after a minute or so. Tried photographing it, but on the silicon sensor there's not much of a difference and so no stand out pix. It's getting dark and there are more and more flashes of green, turquoise and blue in the water, some like exploding fireworks, others whipping across the water like lightning. Decided not to stay up late and try and shoot the biolum, have to cross Hecate Strait in the morning. I want to get there on time. Jake is expecting me for dinner—with the halibut.

May 25 05:04

About two hours ago or so, Lir jumped on my chest, back arched, ears raised, hissing, tail wagging (a sign of an angry cat). After a day on the ocean, you fall into a deep, deep sleep. When Lir jumped on me, he didn't wake me up right away, but the hissing and the claw nagging on my left shoulder eventually got through my slumber. I lifted my head. Lir's wide eyes were in my face were staring into mine, his hot breath on my nose and cheeks. I was still a bit groggy when Lir leapt off my chest and

2

raced up the gangway from the focsle, stopping at the top of the stairs, continuing to hiss. Something must be up. I grabbed the headlamp I always keep under the pillow, put it on and switched on the ultra-bright LED. Lir whipped around and headed up the stairs, then aft to the cabin door. I pulled myself up the stairs. The LED swept the upper part of the darkened cabin, the wheel, engine controls, radar and GPS turned off, the VHF radio always tuned to a red LED display of Channel one six, the stove, the table, the benches. Nothing out of the ordinary. Lir stood at the doorway that led out to the aft deck. The retina of his wide cat's eyes reflecting bright yellow-white from the headlamp, his back arched, ears raised and twitching, and the fur on his ramrod erect tail at its full bushy extent. Something must really be upsetting Lir, but I couldn't see what. I took the couple of steps to the door. Lir hissed, trying to block the way. "I need to know what's up, Lir," I said, scooping him up. I dropped him behind me on the deck, opened the door and stepped out to see one of the most beautiful sights I had ever seen in my life.

Barnard Harbour, as far as the eye could see, was lit up in a million shades of blue, with flashes of greens, streaks of yellow and occasional blinks of red, purple or orange. I had to look up to see if the ocean was reflecting aurora borealis. The sky was crystal clear with brilliant stars.

The colours weaved and twirled, faded and brightened. I had the thought that it was like something from a movie special effects team assigned to create an alien seascape.

I stood there, mesmerized—only that old word fits. I stared at the ever-changing blue light. Shimmering, pulsing turquoise. Predator! Danger! For a fleeting moment—no more than a couple of seconds—that turquoise triggered an instant of pure panic. My heart raced as my reptilian brain warned of some old, no *ancient*, predatory menace. *Flee*, the reptilian brain ordered. My forebrain overruled. The beauty enchanted me, as the turquoise faded and the vision ranged moment by moment from a dull grey blue through hundreds of shades to bright royal blue and dark navy. Lir screeched and batted my ankle. I didn't move. Lir gently love-scratched my ankle.

"What's wrong, Lir?" I asked. "This is so beautiful." But the cat's actions had woken me up. I remembered what my day job was, went back into the cabin and grabbed my gear.

I set up the tripod on the dock—it was a steadier platform than the boat. I first recorded establishing shots and then close ups with the video camera. I "locked off" the video camera, just letting it run, and began walking up and down the dock, taking stills at various angles and focal lengths.

I heard drumming. Far off, but not so faint that it seemed to echo off the mountains. I guessed that somewhere, on a boat, perhaps on shore, someone else had seen the biolum and was celebrating with drumming, but what kind? At first it sounded like First Nations' drumming. Perhaps someone or a group of people were on one of the islands. Then it was like a snare drum, then a marching band bass drum, then First Nations' again, then Japanese kodo, then it faded, to be replaced by a haunting woman's voice singing, but so distant I couldn't make it out. Or was it a male tenor? I wasn't sure. That too faded away. I decided that someone on a boat far off had a big sound system on board, and since sound travels faster at night that was what I was hearing. In that moment, I felt exhausted and knew I should go back to bed.

I carried the camera gear back on board to stow it in the cabin. I noticed that small puddles and water drops covered the deck. It had been dry earlier. The water appeared blue, a much lighter shade of biolum blue, given the small amount on the deck. How did it get there? There was no wind. The lapping waves were not enough to push the water up on board. Lir sat at the cabin door. As I approached the door, the cat actually sneered at me, in disgust. Or so I thought.

It was then I dropped the tripod I had been carrying under my armpit. It fell to the deck into one of the puddles with a bit of a splash. I went into the cabin and stowed the camera gear. Lir followed, sniffed, mewed, stretched and headed down to the focsle. I returned to the deck, bent down to pick up the tripod. Water dripped onto my hands. Sea water with the salty smell, but it had the faint trace of a perfume, perhaps rose petals. For a second, the water on my hand glowed a faint blue and then the glow disappeared.

I stowed the tripod and returned to my bunk. Lir lay stretched out on his back, asleep on the opposite bunk. I fell asleep in seconds.

09:15

I carry a satellite adapter for my smart phone—I am paying for the bandwidth anyway, although I have a minimum plan—so I decided to do some basic Google researching. Only a few referenced to bioluminescent displays at Barnard Harbour, mostly by adventure guides or their tourist clients. I searched coastal First Nations oral history, myths or legends on bioluminescence or ocean lights, but came up with nothing on Google or on Google Scholar. Not that an empty search means much. After a century of exploitation, appropriation with others profiting from stories, much has been held back for good reasons.

That sparse search result for both the phenomenon and the First Nations' references meant that I had the makings of a good and exclusive story.

10:05

I'm getting the *Ogygia* ready to cross Hecate Strait, doing all the routine maintenance and safety checks. Warm, late May morning, scattered clouds. Strangely silent this morning, you should hear the distant barking of the sea lions that roost on the rocks outside the harbour inlet. The only sounds are the occasional caw caw of a gull and the slight breeze in the conifers. I look out toward Whale Channel and Gil Island. The salt chuck is its usually grey green, but the bioluminescence is still there even in daylight—fingers of indigo blue reaching from the harbour all the way to Whale Channel.

11:13 05-25(SMS Text via satellite service)

Jake. Leaving Barnard in a minute. Weather fine. May be bit late. Good photo ops en route. Plan late supper. Keirahn.

14:00

Passing south of Campania Island into Caamaño Sound. No whales sighted, so far. Strange streaks of royal blue in the ocean are getting stronger, as I begin to head west toward Hecate Strait.

14:45

Anchoring for lunch south of the Dewdney and Glide Island Eco reserve. Saw what was probably a humpback blowing to the south towards Aristazabal Island. Lir is still upset, pacing the aft deck. Not happy at all. If this keeps up, may have to put him in his carrier until we reach Haida Gwaii. Relaxing afternoon, sea calm, soft breeze, warm day. I could stay here all day, if I didn't have to be in Queen Charlotte City tonight.

16:35

I must have drifted to sleep, probably because I was up most of the night. A sharp, stinging pain in my lower thigh (I wore shorts) and catfight screeching from Lir woke me. At first, I thought he had attacked me, but the cat's scream came from the stern. There, in full fighting mode, Lir hissed and pawed at a length of strange, light-blue and grey-speckled seaweed. At least I think that's what it was. A branch of that seaweed glistened on the deck, on the same spot where I had lain down and drifted off. Perhaps that was what had stung me.

I pulled myself up and kicked it out of the way. Lir screeched and raked his claws over a branch. I wasn't sure what it was, so I pulled out the fishing gloves stored beside the rods, almost full finger, with just the tips exposed. I grabbed the seaweed—or whatever it was; it squirmed when I picked it up—and tossed it overboard.

Some water dripped down on my fingertips and wrists. It smelled fishy and of sea salt, combined with that faint scent of roses again.

I checked where that seaweed or whatever-it-was had stung me. Barely noticeable. A tiny red spot. To be safe, I triple disinfected it, first with an alcohol wipe, then a dab of hydrogen peroxide, and finally some antibiotic cream.

If I am going to make it to Queen Charlotte City, then I better get a move on. So, turned on the engines and went forward to winch up the anchor. The boat had drifted into one of the streaks of blue, or else the streaks of blue had drifted toward us while I was anchored.

Looked over the side. Some spindly filaments of that blue stuff stuck to the hull. Should wash off when I get up to speed. Likely won't get to Queen Charlotte now until the early hours of tomorrow.

16:45

Can't get a satellite uplink to text Jake. I'll be really late. Will try again in Hecate Strait, away from the islands. Not sure why, but something in my head tells me it's something I must do.

16:55

Going to increase speed a bit more across Hecate Strait to make up for lost time. Want to get to Haida Gwaii. Just under 100 nautical miles at 15 knots, heading 286 or close to west northwest. Should take me seven hours, arriving just after midnight. Too late for dinner. It's been a bit of long day, but I feel great. Must have been the nap.

20:35

What the fuck? What happened to me? I am still off Banks Island. I should be halfway to Haida Gwaii by now. Must turn due west. Get across Hecate Strait to Haida Gwaii.

20:40

Course correction made. I'm hearing that drumming again. Close. I look around, check the radar, but no vessels on the scope. Drumming getting louder, a driving rhythm. The drums echo off the distant island mountains and echo back again. Thousands of drums, in unison, each beating out something incredibly old, back to my ancient hominid ancestors and a hollow log. No. Perhaps even older, going back to some tiny proto-mammal, its paws beating a tree branch in panic at the approach of a reptilian predator. I look at Lir. He's still pacing the deck, clearly agitated. Increasing speed to 20 knots, the maximum tolerance for this old boat. I have to get away from the drums.

May 26 11:35

I woke up about an hour ago, naked, on my bunk in the focsle. Sleeping bag soaked in cold, clammy sweat. I am exhausted. Also feeling absolutely wonderful. And a bit buzzed? Am I high on something? Haven't eaten since 17:00 yesterday, but I am not hungry. I fumbled into my jeans then pulled myself up to the helm and checked the GPS. At least it's working. Fuck! I am back where I started yesterday, where Caamaño Sound opens into Hecate Strait, a bit southwest of the eco reserve. *Ogygia* is barely moving. The GPS shows the boat drifting slowly northward directly for Aranzazu Banks, a mid-ocean shoal, depth ranging from 50 feet to 120 feet at its height. No problem. I pulled myself out on the aft deck. Lir was sleeping on the stern. I looked over the side.

Ogygia is caught in one of those royal blue currents. It is that current that is pushing the boat toward Aranzazu. It's a beautiful clear day. Banks Island is bright in the sun, with the dark olive green of its forest cover. Ahead of me is fog over Aranzazu Banks.

I checked the track on the GPS. From 2040 until 2054 I was heading due west at 20 knots. Then at 2055, I slowed back down to ten knots, reversed course for ten minutes, then southeast, slowing down to three knots, then cutting engines at 2119 and then drifting.

Why?

What's happening to me? What's happening to my mind? Why I am doing this?

Lir meowed, "Feed me."

I grabbed some dry food and emptied it in his bowl. He started to devour it, looked up me, with a contemptuous turned up nose and then kept eating.

I put the burner on to boil water for tea. Then I heard the

drumming again. Faint, far off, and right ahead. Across the water came haunting music. It faded, and then returned sort of like when a car radio gets out of range of a transmitter. In those few moments, the music was clear. It somehow lured, enticed, seduced me.

I grabbed my mug of tea, sat down at the helm. Ahead of me, the fog over Aranzazu Banks seemed to be lifting. It seems there is an island there. What? I checked the GPS. No island. Just a shoal with a high point 50 feet below the waves.

I remembered last night. I was heading west, 20 knots, *Ogygia* smashing and bouncing, as it hit each wave at that speed. Then I pulled back the sticks, slowing the boat down. I couldn't stop myself, even though part of my mind was screaming "No!" It was something I had to do. Part of my mind said, "Don't! Keep going to Haida Gwaii!" A mental gate slammed shut, silencing that part of my mind. I turned the boat 180 degrees back to the east. Ahead of me, I could see the shimmering bright blue and blue-green and silver-blue with its streaks of red and green and yellow. I changed course, pulling back the sticks, slowing down every few minutes. Then the boat reached the edge of the bright blue. I cut the engines. The boat bobbed for a moment, and then turned north, the bright blue current slowly pulling it.

The drumming began, low and steady.

I left the helm, opened the cabin door. I felt twenty years old again. Blue shimmering lights flickered and pulsed up from the ocean in time to the drumbeat. Streaks of light over the boat, flashing and twirling with the tempo. In the late May chill on Hecate Strait, I took off my shirt. I whirled and danced and leapt up and down. The stern of the boat bounced in counter-rhythm to my movements.

Somehow, I kicked off my jeans and underwear, and danced naked on the aft of my small boat. Hot, sticky-sweaty. For a moment, a thousand men, ancient warriors, in a dance of ritual ecstasy, surrounded me. Then they were gone, and I wanted them to return.

The drumbeat quickened. I leapt and whirled and bent backwards and forwards. The more I danced, the better I felt. All my worries, all my anxieties, all my low-level depression——gone! I have never felt so strong, so passionate, so confident. At one point, I danced with a blue-green snake, weaving and twisting in time to the drums. The snake came closer, caressed my chest and my thighs, then pulled back, danced with me, and then withdrew and slid back overboard.

What was left of my rational mind squeezed itself through a crack in that gate and said, "Google Tarantella." Then the gate shut again and I was commanded, "Don't. It doesn't matter, Keirahn. Everything is fine."

I remember putting my hands on the gunwales, kicking my legs up and down, screaming at the top of my lungs. At that point, the boat caught a wave. I almost tumbled backwards, overboard. But I was stopped. Stopped by two cold, wet, smooth, incredibly strong tentacles that grabbed me, pinning my arms to my side. I looked down. They were bright blue with filaments of ever-changing colours. I shuddered. The primeval fear of the predator.

The tentacles tightened, fastening my arms against my chest. I tried to escape. I panicked. The scales, electrifying, erotic—if they were scales—somehow connected with the nerves of my hot, sweaty skin. I could no longer move. I gasped. Barely, grabbed a breath. Afraid.

The connection to those scales also felt intoxicatingly erotic. Within that vice-like grip, I writhed with pleasure, desire and fear.

The tentacles pushed me off the gunwale and then gently, ever so gently, deposited me on the deck. I felt and knew its love. The drumming continued. I pulled myself up and danced myself to exhaustion. I crawled to the door, opened it, and crossed the cabin to crawl down the gangway to the focsle bunks. I pulled myself into the sleeping bag and blacked out.

12:15

I found a bottle of single malt scotch at the back of the galley pantry by the sink drain to the holding tank. I'd completely forgotten about it, a leftover from that disastrous birthday party five years ago. About half the bottle remained. I don't usually drink, but I think a glass or two might help me calm down.

13:30
I am just a bit drunk. But my head is clear. Clear*er*.

16:15
Fuck. I got to write this down. Have to. It's not just me that's a little drunk. It's a thing in my head. It's drunk as well. Like a nasty drunk in a bar. That thing—no *things*—in my head are saying they're in command of my body, telling me that they now control my thoughts. What are they? Who are they? I know somehow this began with just one. In that dance last night, they became many. They are now on the way to my brain.

The scotch is wearing off. Can I stop them? How can I stop them if I don't know what they are? For some reason, I know I must save the booze that is left. I am hiding it under the personal flotation devices in the safety locker.

May 27 08:12
Lir woke me up, screeching, demanding to be fed.

Last night I danced with a lover that truly loves me. As I heard the drumming, I became more and more impatient for I knew that soon I would no longer be so lonely. After so many years, I would find love again. Yes, Lir, I love you too. I will find the food for you.

When was the last time I fed you?

I don't know.

It could have been two days ago.

09:10
Lir is fed, gobbling up a whole can of cat food. It must have been a wild night. My mobile is smashed, in pieces on the deck. I don't know where the SAT adapter went. I think I threw it overboard. Both VHF radios are gone, ripped from the housing.

What about the scotch?

"Throw them overboard," my lover had told me. "You

don't need them any longer."

The GPS and radar are still working.

"You will stay safe, until I can come to you," my lover said.

I wrench open the safety locker, breaking the doorknob. In a panic, I grab the PFDs and lifejackets; throw them over my shoulder. The bottle is still there. I chug the fiery liquid. My head clears a bit.

Lir has finished eating. Now, he's sitting on the deck, staring at me, with a low, challenging purr.

It's hard to describe how wonderful last night was. The sky flashing green, blue, white as if there were fireworks going off continuously for hours. The sea, bright blue, emerald green, leafy green, indigo, royal purple, different waves all of different shades.

He came aboard? She came aboard? They came aboard?

Drumming, always the drumming, but a softer, steadier beat. Far off, a woman sang a love song, a song of seduction.

He came, a beautiful young man with long hair mixed with seaweed. He pulled himself on board on the port side. He had the torso of a man and the lower body of a seal. As he reached the deck, the seal flippers became legs. All while a woman—or women?—sang those haunting love songs.

She came on board at the starboard side. Both held me, whispering, dissolving all my loneliness, all the pain, all the hurt from life. The Siren grabbed my left hand and brought it to her mouth. Sharp teeth bit into my fingers, drawing blood. The pain, the dripping red, only made me want more. She smiled—there were no fangs as I expected in that moment—then slipped over the side.

The Selkie remained. He embraced me, kissed me, made love to me. Then he too was gone.

The drumming grew louder, more urgent. Once again, I danced with—what? Ribbons of light? Tentacles? Snakes? Gods? Spirits? Ghosts? Ancient warriors leaping and wielding spears? An exotic twirling Medusa with a crown of writhing blue tentacles? I have never experienced anything like that. I wanted it to go on forever. To never stop. I grew tired. Once again, I staggered down to my bunk to sleep until Lir woke me.

"Feed me! Feed me."

13:15

I must have slipped on the wet stairs going down to the focsle. I blacked out. Perhaps I have a mild concussion. My head is clear. Soon those things in my head will recover, take me over again, control me forever. They are not lovers. They are temptation, they are a symbiotic part of a creature that intrigues, seduces, enraptures, and bewitches. All so it can feed, feed on whatever creature it has trapped.

Lir is on the seat beside the helm. He looks up at me with big eyes. His meows are like someone crying. Shit! Lir! Where's the bottle of scotch? How much is left?

15:10

Lir. I must save Lir. I grabbed him, put him in his carrier. I head east at 20 knots. I have found the bottle of scotch. I take a sip. It will keep it/them from fully controlling me. When the scotch is gone, I'm doomed. But if I drop Lir on an island, he might survive. Another sip of the scotch. Not much left in the bottle. I have to go back. I have to go back to Aranzazu Banks. My heart already aches. I can't stand being lonely anymore. I want to feel that over whelming all-encompassing love.

15:32

Getting closer now to the islands. I have pulled up the GPS and charts, looking for a safe place to drop Lir onshore. There appears to be a small inlet on Barnard Island where I can get in. Tide is right, falling. I can get right into shore before the tide turns. I drain the last of the scotch from the bottle.

I want to turn around now. Go back to Aranzazu Banks and find peace. Lir meows softly in his carrier. That love for my cat drives me on.

15:59

Coming in shore now. I have to go back. No, I can't.

Desperately, I lick the last drops from the edge of the bottle and the bottle cap. Is it enough to let me finish? I'm going to download the log onto a memory stick, put Lir's collar on and attach the stick with a zip tie, that way people may know what is happening to me. I'll take him up to the tree line, put down the carrier and leave the door open. Video. Fuck! That thing stopped me from recording what happened the past couple of days. The dash cam is still working. I rig my two helmet cameras. One of them pointing aft to the deck, the second inside the cabin, covering the helm,

I have to go. I have to get back. He is calling. She is calling. Love is calling.

I now return for that promised ultimate love. The end of my loneliness. But am I lonely or is it an illusion? I don't know. Is it true? Or is all this a dream, a nightmare, a hallucination? In the next few hours I will know. Or perhaps I won't. All I know is that I have no choice.

15 November
SECRET

TO: MAJOR CRIMES E DIVISION
CC. COAST GUARD PRINCE RUPERT

FROM: SGT. CYNTHIA HUDSON OFFICER IN CHARGE, QUEEN CHARLOTTE CITY DETACHMENT

SUBJECT: MISSING PERSON KEIRAHN TAKAYUKI McMONAGLE

On 10 November, a tour guide came to the detachment to report that on 8 November, while escorting a party of photographers, one of them using a telephoto lens, spotted a cat on the shores of Barnard Island. After determining it was safe to bring the boat into the area, a shore party landed nearby and was able to find and retrieve the cat. The cat was relatively healthy. Although it did show signs of a rough life in the bush, it had obviously successfully lived off the land for some considerable period of time. Once the cat was on board, the party found that it had a collar. Attached to the collar with zip ties was a memory stick that was small enough as to not interfere with the cat's movements.

On reaching Queen Charlotte City, the cat was taken to a local veterinary clinic for a check-up which revealed that the cat had a pet identification chip. The scan revealed the registered owner was missing person KEIRAHN TAKAYUKI McMON-AGLE. The veterinarian then advised them to contact this detachment. At that time, they handed in the memory stick.

We informed McMONAGLE's cousin JAKE GARAGAN, in Sandspit, of the discovery of the cat, since, in a small community, such information doesn't remain secret for long. The log entries were not encrypted and were easy to download. Transcripts are attached to this report. Due to the nature of the log entries, we are withholding that information and recommend it remain secret until a proper investigation can be carried out. We have also advised GARAGAN that a Cormorant search and rescue helicopter from CFB Comox will sweep over the area on Barnard Island in the next few days, but it is unlikely that McMONAGLE survived a storm later on the night of May 27. Any recovery operation will have to wait until spring as the weather is rapidly deteriorating.

The cat named LIR is now happily at home with next of kin GARAGAN, although at least two people who had been on the boat had expressed an interest in adoption, if no family was located.

19 August
TOP SECRET CANADIAN EYES ONLY

TO: COMMISSIONER ROYAL CANADIAN MOUNT-ED POLICE
CHIEF OF DEFENCE STAFF
MINISTER OF PUBLIC SAFETY
MINISTER OF NATIONAL DEFENCE
FROM: COMMANDING OFFICER RCMP E DIVISION
CC E DIVISION MAJOR CRIMES COMMAND, DIGI-

Aranzazu Banks

TAL FORENSICS, COASTAL PATROL, QUEEN CHAR-
LOTTE CITY, COAST GUARD PRINCE RUPERT

SUBJECT: MISSING PERSON KEIRAHN TAKAYUKI
RYAN McMONAGLE

Senior officers of E Division have now viewed the three
partially restored videos on the memory cards recovered by
RCMP divers from the wreck of the OGYGIA on 5 June; ap-
proximately one year after the vessel was lost.

We have decided, given the circumstances, to inform the
family—first cousin JAKE GARAGAN, of Sandspit, (who filed
the original missing persons report) and father HIDEO
McMONAGLE of Langley—that a "freak wave" in the storm
hit the boat later on May 27. KIERAHN McMONAGLE,
therefore, had no chance of survival. The actual circumstances
of his death are to remain top secret, Canadian Eyes Only.

Every effort should be made during the operation to recover DNA from any remains of the creature for purposes of
analysis.

We have searched classified summaries in other jurisdic-
tions. They all indicate similar stories, ranging back to ancient

history, may (repeat may) be based on this creature. They make mention of Sirens (of Greek Legend), Morgens (of Welsh and Breton tradition), as well as Selkie and Kelpie (of Irish and Scottish mythologies). The only discrepancy is that they refer to humanoid beings. We have yet to reconcile this information with our findings.

Since there are no previous written records of the creature in North America, it can be classified as an invasive species and subject to immediate eradication. This is the legal basis for the operation.

The creature is definitely a hazard to navigation and human beings on the ocean. Senior officers at Canadian Forces MARPAC (Maritime Command Pacific) recommend that a search and destroy operation be tasked in November to eradicate the creature.

The cover story will be that a rough weather live fire naval exercise will be conducted in the region from Aranzazu Banks to the Block Islands where the OGYGIA sank. MARPAC informs confidentially that the US Navy has requested a joint training exercise. USN wants this to take place during rough weather so they can test communications, navigation, and weapons systems. MARPAC believes we can oblige the Americans and let them test their weapons (as well as our own weapons and interoperability) without telling them why we have chosen that spot.

Aranzazu Banks

The videos somewhat confirm the events that McMONAGLE described in his log entry, which we recovered from the memory stick fastened to the collar of his cat, LIR. This is the same cat the civilians rescued last fall on the shores of Barnard Island.

The video shows how McMONAGLE died.

Once McMONAGLE left the cat LIR at Oswald Bay on Barnard Island, he takes the time to set up two small portable video cameras, one over the door to the cabin, covering the aft deck, and a second inside the door covering the cabin and focsle. This was in addition to the dash cam. (Note: divers were unable to locate and recover any of McMONAGLE's professional video and photo gear where images might confirm the early logs. It may be that he threw the gear overboard at the same as the radio. Thus, it is impossible to say how much of his experience, starting at Barnard Harbour, was real and how much was an induced hallucination).

He traveled back to Aranzazu Banks and cut the engines, letting the boat drift. He then stripped naked and sat, waiting, on a small portable folding canvas campstool. He was smiling and appeared relaxed.

At time code 18:17:09, the forward-looking dash cam records a series of long, royal blue, grey speckled, snake-like tentacles approaching the boat. The aft looking camera records at 18:18:56, nine of the tentacles, each about the width of a man's arm reaching over the side of the boat, and on to the deck, three on the port side, three on the starboard side and three from the stern.

McMONAGLE was smiling and reached out with open arms to greet the tentacles. All nine begin to caress him, until he eventually fell back onto the deck. All the time he was smiling and moaning softly in a form of ecstasy. According to video time code, this continued until about 18:39:22 at which time, close up enhancement shows, all nine tentacles released a thin sharp spike from their tips. The spikes penetrated his skin at various points and pulsed, probably injecting substances into the man's bloodstream.

At this point, McMONAGLE was somewhat semi-conscious but apparently still aware of his surroundings. He was still smiling. At 1841, enhanced audio showed that he whispers, "Thank you, oh thank you," and then "This is so wonderful, thank you." It is our conclusion that the tentacles injected McMONAGLE with a naturally produced muscle relaxant, a painkiller of some kind, a hallucinogen and possibly a blood agent, likely an anticoagulant.

At 18:50:34 the nine tentacles withdrew back into the ocean, leaving McMONAGLE spread eagled on the deck, looking up at the sky and still in a state of ecstasy.

At 19:02:05, four much-larger tentacles, two port and two starboard, came over the side of the boat. Close up enhancement shows that the end of each tentacle had a round, toothed mouth, and a triangular shaped tongue with a spike at its forward edge. The spiked tongue penetrated both his hands and his feet. Then his flesh and bone slowly began to dissolve. Each tentacle continued to slowly consume his arms and legs, moving upward to the torso. The tentacles enlarged in the same manner of a python. It appears that McMONAGLE is still alive at this point because he lifts his head, smiling, and watches as his arms and legs being consumed.

That process ends at 19:19:33, when the tentacles reach the shoulders and hips. There is some evidence of blood on the deck of the boat. McMONAGLE closed his eyes and relaxed, likely losing consciousness from continued blood loss.

At this point, the creature no longer needed McMON-AGLE's acquiescence, cooperation, or consent. It became more aggressive, tearing and ripping at his torso and then sucking in the dissolved flesh. Note: that at the beginning of this process, McMONAGLE was likely still alive. Four more tentacles came on the boat and joined the others in a frenzy of consumption. Most of his body is gone by 19:25:00, except for the head. One tentacle enlarged and swallowed his head whole at 19:26:13.

All eight tentacles then entered the cabin, and in doing so, as recorded by the interior video, caused considerable damage. All withdrew at 19:45:12, leaving the boat adrift.

We believe they were in search of other prey.

At 20:39:00, the weather changed, and a westerly wind

picked up, beginning to drive the OGYGIA eastward. The dash cam video and the deck video, both still operating at that point, recorded the large bright blue 'fingers' in the water that still surrounded the boat.

By 21:00:00, the storm overcame the twilight was almost at full force. The boat was rolling in heavy waves. picked up and All The blue elements in the ocean disappeared simultaneously. By 21:50:00, the wind became a full gale and, nearing the end of their battery life, all cameras stopped operating.

As previously reported, the storm drove OGYGIA on to the rocks of the Block Islands, between Banks Island and Trutch Island, where it sank.

After the cat LIR's rescue and the analysis of the memory stick's information, a search and recovery operation began this spring. As in the previous report (see attached), An enforcement aircraft from the Department of Fisheries and Oceans spotted the wreck in clear water at an unusually low tide. All parties involved consider this a lucky find.

Investigators showed a carefully edited version of the video to scientists at both the University of British Columbia and Simon Fraser University. To avoid wild stories on social media, detectives tused the cover story of an investigation into fraud and theft of intellectual property in the special effects industry. The majority of interviewees concluded that the creature was "modelled" on the jellyfish by how its tentacles captured, stung, dissolved and consumed its prey. Some sources noted how the largest known jellyfish are about 100 to 200 centimetres in the "bell" with tentacles. Depending on the species, that can range from 90 centimetres to two metres. The other "model" sea creature is the cuttlefish, which uses bioluminescent displays to attract prey.

It is likely that the creature is in a symbiotic relationship with a parasite that can take over a mind. That's only supposed to happen to insects and fishes. If that is the case, the first tentacle prick injected a single parasite into the blood stream. Somehow that microscopic parasite crossed the blood-brain barrier. Once in the brain, it became active. The parasite gets nutrients and oxygen from blood. It grows; it takes over the brain neuron by neuron.

On land, the spider is one Arthropod that stings, then floods the body of the prey with digestive enzymes and then sucks the bodily fluids.

Given the video evidence it is unlikely that anyone, whether ancient Greek or modern mariner survived the encounter.

Centre Ice

By Caitlin Marceau

The bell rings. Jérôme, smiling, approaches the counter where an old woman stands. Her hair tumbles around her face in thinning grey waves, shockingly long for her age. Eclectically adorned, she wears a worn sheepskin coat with elastic-wasted jeans and poinsettia red galoshes, which leave watery footprints behind her, trailing to the front door.

"Mme. Elodi, you're out late. How's the rain?" the young man asks, eyes looking past her to the plaque hanging in the arena's foyer.

"Wet, mostly," she jokes, smiling as she leans against the wooden countertop. "It's come down hard enough that the blueberry fields are practically swimming, but thankfully the season for them is practically over."

He nods in silent agreement, but when he doesn't say anything back, she sighs and offers more.

"It's not good, but I've seen worse. It rained so hard in '88 that the library roof caved in and ruined the entire reference section. But tonight isn't nearly as bad as it was then. Besides,

22

the rain shouldn't be what's on your mind. Not with it being your last day here!"

"It's not," he says, good cheer returning to his face. "I'm going to be working through the fall again."

Jérôme beams, unable to hide his enthusiasm at the thought of working with Les Sangliers for another season. Unlike the kids who ran the snack bar before him, he didn't have any plans to move, visit family, or attend another school at the end of summer.

Although he'd considered sending applications out to the bigger rinks in Québec—or even one in the neighbouring Saguenay-Lac-Saint-Jean townships—for the upcoming season, his chances of getting selected would improve with two years experience here, so Jérôme decided to remain the town's favourite snack man for the foreseeable future.

"Very good! Édouard must be thrilled," she says.

Jérôme shrugs, not wanting to confess that she's dead wrong. Saying his father wasn't happy about his job at the rink was an understatement, but he'd long since given up on that argument.

"Now," the woman says, pulling him from his thoughts and a fiver from her purse, "would you be so kind as to get me a box of chocolate raisins?"

"Of course!"

"How's work been treating you here, dear?" she asks, taking her raisins and tossing a toonie from her change in the plastic tip jar.

"Good! I'm excited to start school tomorrow, although I hope I get an easy English teacher who doesn't give me too much homework. I don't want to be stuck reading books I don't care about when I could be spending time here."

"You enjoy being at the arena?"

"Love it. Sometimes, I don't want to leave."

"You sound just like your uncle."

"I wouldn't know. I guess you knew him?" he asks, eyes wandering to the entrance of the building once more.

"We go way back, yes."

She gives him a small smile and looks at her watch. Satisfied that he's no longer worrying about the rain, it's clear she's no longer interested in the conversation.

She begins to shuffle towards the doors of the stadium.

"Sorry, Mme. Elodie, but may I ask what you're doing here? The arena is about to close."

"The arena is open late tonight, sweetie. Didn't Maxime tell you? There's a town meeting after closing hours today."

"I guess he forgot to mention it. Why aren't you using the town hall to meet, if you don't mind me asking?"

"Young man, have you ever been in the old building?"

Jérôme shakes his head.

"You're lucky then. It's like the walls suck out any sunshine, even when the windows are open, and the lights buzz like flies in their sockets. If you listen closely at night, you can hear bats fluttering in the attic and the ground shifting beneath the building. It's only a matter of time before that old thing comes crashing down. I don't intend to be trapped inside it when it finally does. Do you?"

"No way. No ma'am."

She winks at him and enters the seating area as a few more elderly people walk through the front doors, through the lobby, and past his concessions counter, following Mme. Elodie into the rink.

"Jérôme, could you clean the plaque please?" his boss calls from the door of his office, only a few feet away.

"Sure thing!"

He puts a small plastic sign on the counter—BACK IN 5— and grabs a small bottle of all purpose spray and a rag before making his way to the arena's entrance.

He stares at the sign on the wall, bright gold mounted on rich mahogany, and runs a bare hand over the name on display.

Théo Brodeur.

His uncle.

He squirts some of the light pink liquid onto the sign and rubs the cleanser into the wood and metal, removing whatever dust and grime may have collected on the plaque since he'd polished it the night before. He knows the outline of the words well, having felt them under his fingers every night since starting at the arena. Cleaning the sign had become such an easy task that he let his eyes wander to the bust of his uncle, locked safely with his ashes behind glass in the arena wall.

A lifetime ago his dad's older brother, Théo, had single-handedly broken the local team's 27-year losing streak, much to the town's amazement. He brought home trophies the villagers of Sainte-Élisabeth-de-Proulx had only ever prayed for in hushed voices, and he put *Les Sangliers* back on the map for junior hockey. Everyone thought he was going to make it big, and he would have, had he not been one of the victims of a landslide that had killed eight people in '67. While his life had been cut tragically short, the luck (and winning streak) Théo had brought *Les Sangliers* lived on.

He gives the plaque one last pass before returning to his post at the counter, and soon the pillars of his community begin to saunter in—his principal, the town mayor, the chief librarian—followed by some of the farming community. The door to the arena opens again, but this time his father is the one slumping towards the stadium doors, eyes glued to the heels of the people ahead of him.

"Dad!" Jérôme shouts in surprise.

The man freezes in his tracks, stopping so suddenly that the woman behind him only narrowly avoids crashing into his back. Instead of an angry huff or disparaging look, she pats him on the back and continues into the arena behind the long line of people.

"Dad?"

Édouard drags his feet to the counter, his dirty work boots leaving scuff marks and mud on the tiled floor behind him. He plays with the drawstrings that hang from the front of his coat, not looking to meet his son's smile. His gainsborough hair, what little there is left, was matted against his forehead, and his plaid shirt was misbuttoned. Although he'd never been known for being a sharp dresser, it was unusual for Édouard to look so bedraggled in public.

"Dad, what are you doing here? You never care about this kind of stuff."

His father nods, but doesn't say anything.

Jérôme leans against the edge of the counter, brushing imaginary dirt from the clean service window.

"Why did you come out this time? It's raining."

25

Centre Ice

He grunts in reply, running a sweaty palm across the front of his jacket to dry his skin, shifting his weight from foot to foot. He's quiet, and the unusual silence concerns Jérôme.

"Dad, is everything okay? You hate the rain. Why did you come out tonight?" His dad shakes his head, opening and closing his mouth a bunch of times as he avoids his son's concerned stare.

Jérôme reaches out and puts a comforting hand on his dad's shoulder.

Édouard relents and looks up, eyes sunken and red with exhaustion. Determined, he opens his mouth.

"Jérôme, can I see you in the players' room? I need your help," Maxime interrupts.

"Sure thing," he answers with uncertainty. "I'll see you soon, Dad."

He waves goodbye to his father before Maxime leads him into the maze of hallways that lead to the player's room. It soon becomes obvious that while the foyer of the building has been modernized, the hidden passageways of the arena have seen no such love. The tunnels smell musty and of decay, spotted with mould and flecks of chipped paint. Dirt and grime line the ground, thick in the corners between where the walls and the cement floor meet. In a room off the main path, metal drags against stone and—for the first time since applying for the job—nervousness seizes Jérôme.

In the heart of the town, the building has always been a point of pride. Constructed in 1943, it is the only historic site in the area left standing, and one of the few buildings that the community maintained.

Or so he thought.

"I'm surprised the building looks this... old," Jérôme says, his voice bouncing off the corridors until the silence at the end of the hall absorbs it.

"It always looks like this at the end of the season," Maxime replies. "By the time another one starts, it'll look good as new. We just need to breathe some life into the place."

As the players' room comes into view, anticipation quickly replaces his shiver of anxiety. The space is normally off-limits to non-team members. Jérôme can't help but walk so closely

26

behind his boss that he nearly steps on his heels. His heart has never beat so fast, blood pumping with excitement to finally see the spot where *Les Sangliers* prepare to do battle on the ice.

As he enters, a set of strong hands reach out and grab him, pinning his arms to his side.

"Hey! What the—"

Maxime picks up a thick bundle of rope and begins wrapping it carefully around Jérôme.

"Very funny, guys. You got me. I don't really get the joke, but good job," he says, trying to laugh it off.

Maxime pulls the cord hard, letting it dig into the young man's skin. When his boss doesn't laugh, he begins to panic.

Maxime continues securing the boy's arms to his sides as Jérôme yells for help, trying to fight against the bonds. He lands a kick on the man's kneecap, and there's an audible *pop!* as something important dislodges from place.

"Osti d' tabarnak de câlice de criss de marde!"

The blow isn't enough to knock him down, and after Maxime is done roping Jérôme up, the two men carry him out of the players' room and onto the ice.

The townsfolk and community leaders sit in the stands around the rink. When they see Jérôme carried out, a hush falls over the crowd before swelling into a cacophony of cheers and clapping. Some of them even stomp their feet on the ground, the echoes thundering through the arena. They leer at Jérôme from their seats. A ravenous, animalistic energy pulsates around them.

They bring Jérôme closer to a giant hole, freshly bored into the centre of the rink.

The two men place Jérôme face up onto the ice and begin waving to the crowd. The boy writhes away from the hole, worming his body back to the locker room, but he stops when he sees a man stepping onto the rink.

Uncle Théo.

He glides towards Jérôme, footsteps silent on the cold surface, and the crowd goes wild, pumping their fists and whistling at the town's long-extinguished star. Théo, however, is far less enthusiastic than the audience. His gaze is far away and hollow, his shoulders hunched in submission. He wears his hockey pads and uniform, an old fashioned costume in modern times. His dead eyes look past Jérôme and into the ice, looking at something beyond what the others can see.

"It's that time of the year again, ladies and gentlemen," Maxime yells to the crowd, "where we offer up another sacrifice to the spirits that guard *Les Sangliers* and brings us another year of success, prosperity, and rejuvenation for our community!"

The crowd claps and continues to stomp their feet in the stands.

"Thank you, Édouard, for granting us this opportunity. We know this can't be easy for you, but we hope you'll find comfort in knowing that, like Théo, Jérôme's spirit will live on and be with us. Always."

Jérôme screams, words spilling from his mouth and forming one desperate plea for freedom. He doesn't understand what's happening or, more aptly, he doesn't want to. He searches the seats for a face he trusts, for someone he knows will help, but even his father in the first row is a stranger to him. He's crying, not just tears of mourning, but tears of joy.

Jérôme looks away from him, but immediately wishes he hadn't. His eyes fall on a row of children standing near the audience. Like Théo, they look hollow and void of emotion. Their posture is slumped and concave, and their sunken eyes stare into the ice. A few of them shiver, cold without bodies to feel the chill in the air. Jérôme recognizes a few of them, but it takes him a second to figure out from where.

The arena.

They're all kids who worked the concession stand.

They're all kids like Jérôme.

"Théo, we hope this gives you the energy to have a great hockey year, and that our team can enjoy another lucky season," Maxime says. The audience howls with excitement as Édouard rises from his seat, descends the stadium steps, and cautiously steps onto the rink.

Jérôme begins to yell and thrash on the ice, trying to fight against the rope that keeps him immobile, but it's no use. The two men and his father slide Jérôme to the hole and lower him into the narrow opening in the rink.

He screams, but the symphony of the crowd swallows up

what little sound he makes. The opening is narrow and tight, compressing his body and bruising his bones as the men push him below ground. A rib snaps as he's lodged into place, his screaming replaced by strangled gasps for air.

There's a low rumble and long groan, followed by a slow trickle of cold water from above. It soaks through his clothing, fills his ears and nose, and it's not long before it swallows him whole.

The last thing Jérôme hears through the water, as his lungs beg for air and the water freezes around him, encasing him in a tomb of ice, is his dad leading the chant for *Les Sangliers*.

His Cold Coffin

By Tyner Gillies

Now

olin placed his hand on the coffin's smooth, wooden surface and found it cold to the touch, devoid of the life and warmth that had once so filled the person inside it. He looked at the picture of his friend that sat in the centre of the shining surface, blinking away tears that made his vision swim. He had not yet cried over Shane's death, doing his best to be the rock on which his other friends could lean, but now he could not help himself and the tears flowed.

He glanced over his shoulder. Fred, with his heavy, square beard and heavy, square shoulders, stood directly behind him. Fred gazed down fixedly at the toes of his shoes, and he was steady, unmoved by heaving sobs that inflicted so many in the church, but Colin could see the shine of tears in the heavy mat of Fred's reddish beard. Behind Fred, Matthew stood with his hands clasped before him, his head hanging. Slender, narrow-faced, Matthew stood the exact opposite of Fred.

The years since the early days of their youth had taken them hundreds of miles away from each other. Only Shane and Fred had stayed in Vernon, British Columbia—the town where they all grew up. Once a year they all returned to renew their friendship, picking up where they left off without a wrinkle. This reunion, forced together by tragedy, left Colin feeling hollowed out and raw. Shane, who had always been the light in their hard lives, was gone, leaving a cold space in their hearts where he once stood.

Then

"Are you sure this is a good idea?" Colin asked, as he stood on Shane's lawn and looked doubtfully through the view finder of the massive, clunking video camera that Shane had 'borrowed' from the high-school Drama Club.

"No," Matthew and Fred said in unison, their voices pitching up in concern. Fred's voice cracked alarmingly, wavering somewhere between Barry White and the skinny string on a violin.

"It'll be fine," Shane said from where he stood on the roof of his house. "The table will break my fall."

Colin focused the camera on the table, a ramshackle piece of furniture Shane had gotten at a garage sale for a dollar, where it sat on the grassy surface, a few feet from the edge of the house. It didn't look like it would support an empty paper cup, let alone break the fall of a heavy kid who had aspirations of being a wrestling superstar.

"Whatcha you doing?" Colin looked at Matthew, who stood beside him and held the portable phone from Shane's kitchen.

Matthew waggled the phone. "To call an ambulance, when he breaks his neck."

"Good idea." Colin focused the camera on Shane's smiling face.

"Are you sure about this?" Fred asked, adjusting the executioner's mask Shane had convinced him to wear.

"Yeah," Shane said, vigorously slapping both of his own shoulders. "Do it!"

Sighing, Fred gave Shane a shove.

His Cold Coffin

Now

"How are you holding up?" Fred asked Colin. The three of them sat, shoulder to shoulder, in the last pew of the now-empty church.

Colin shrugged. "I'm…" He sniffed loudly to stave off the tears that lurked at the corners of his eyes, and cleared his throat. "I'm getting by." He lifted his head and met Fred's gaze, then looked past to Matthew. "This is hard."

Colin's friends knew that he had found Shane and had called the local RCMP detachment. What Fred and Matthew did not know was that Shane had lain in his grubby little apartment for at least a week before Colin had used the spare key he'd gotten from Shane's mother to let himself in. They also didn't know why Colin had made the journey from Vancouver to see Shane in the first place.

Then

Colin sat in his living room, after a day shift as a patrol sergeant with the Vancouver Police Department, when his phone had rung.

"Hello?" he said.

Silence.

He was about to hang up when he heard a voice, Shane's voice, say his name. "Colin?"

He instantly recognized the voice, having heard it every day from the time he was two until he was twenty. "Shane?" he said. A feeling of guilt gripping him. He had not spoken to Shane in months, so absorbed with his recent promotion and all the things that came with it. "How are you, man? You have a bad connection? 'Cause it sounds like you're far away."

Silence on the line.

Colin thought the call had dropped, when he heard, very faintly, "Colin, I'm sorry." And then nothing.

He looked down at his silent phone. He checked his call log and it showed no recent calls. He tried Shane's phone, but it went unanswered and the voicemail was full.

A chill gripped Colin and it kept its hold as he got off the couch, packed an overnight bag, and drove the five hours to Vernon.

When he arrived at the door to Shane's shitty apartment, spare key in hand, he knew instantly what he would find when he got inside. After more than a decade as a street cop, he knew the smell of a dead body. The hallway outside Shane's unit was thick with it.

He opened the door and a cloud of flies and the stench of decay assaulted him. His experience took over and compelled his feet forward, even though his heart broke with every step. Shane lay in his bed, an inflatable mattress on the floor of the small bedroom. Colin had to clap a hand over his mouth to stop the cry that burbled up his throat.

The bloated body, with torso darkly purple and distended, hands and fingers shriveled and pale. The remains of a foam cone—the tell-tale sign of a drug overdose—circled the open mouth. Where Shane's clear blue eyes had once been were now gaping sockets, and in the depth of those sockets wriggled a white mass of maggots.

The body remained, ripe and rotting, but whatever had made Colin's friend who he was, was long gone. He turned and fled the small, filthy apartment, hurrying away before his barely contained scream escaped.

Hours later, as Colin sat in his truck and watched the coroner's body-removal team push the blanket covered stretcher out the front door of the apartment, something occurred to him. Shane had been dead for a week, maybe more, but Colin had heard his voice on the phone less than ten hours before.

A chill ran up his spine.

Now

He shivered in the church pew.

"Were you able to figure out what the official cause of death was?" Matthew asked.

Colin nodded and gazed at his clasped hands. They all knew

what the answer was going to be, but he spoke it out loud anyway. "Drug overdose."

"I thought he had gone to rehab," Fred said, his baritone voice rumbling from the depths of his beard.

"He did," Matthew said. "Or at least he told me he did."

"He must have relapsed." Colin felt stupid the moment the words left his mouth. Of course he had relapsed. That's how people 'in recovery' died of drug overdoses. He had been a cop long enough to know *how* these things happened.

"I want to know why this happened. I talked to Shane after he got out of rehab and he appeared to be doing well. He had a job, was back in the gym, and was talking about joining a little wrestling company that had seen his demos and seemed interested. He had everything going in the right direction. I don't think he did this on his own."

"What are you saying?" Matthew asked, rocking in his seat, hands dry-washing one another. "Do you think Shane was murdered?"

Colin shrugged. "I'm not saying that someone put the needle in his arm, but I think someone put it in his hand. I want to know who that someone was."

"And then what?" Fred asked, his rumbling voice cracking, as fresh tears leaked into his beard.

Colin blew out a big breath through his nose. "And then I'm going to talk to that person. See what they have to say."

They sat silent for several minutes, each struggling with their own thoughts, wrestling with their memories.

"Shane always stood up for us," Colin said, as one particular memory stung him. "I think it's time we stood up for him."

Then

"Don't look at the dance floor," Fred shouted into Colin's ear over the thumping music hammering out of the towering nightclub speakers.

Of course, Colin looked. "That bitch," he said, when he witnessed the spectacle Fred had hoped to spare him from. Matthew stood beside the small, round bar-table they occupied and slapped his hand against his narrow face.

In the center of the dance floor, Colin's ex-girlfriend, Christine, was grinding her crotch against the leg of a tall, slender, undeniably good-looking guy that Colin recognized from several of his university courses.

"I thought she said she needed some time alone," Colin said, raising his voice to be heard over the music.

"When did you guys break up?" Fred asked, as Christine grabbed the good-looking guy's head and began making out with him.

Colin looked at his watch. "About four hours ago."

"That bitch," Matthews said, his palm still plastered to his cheek.

Shane elbowed between Colin and Fred to set two large, plastic jugs of beer on the table. "What do you all look so pissed about?"

"Dance floor," Fred said, jerking his thumb over his shoulder.

Shane stood on his tip-toes and frowned. "That bitch."

"Exactly," Matthew said, his hand slithering off his face.

Shane quirked his mouth in a thoughtful expression, then picked up one of the pitchers and, without aid of a glass, drained off half of the pale ale in a dozen swallows. "Wait here. I'll be back." He slipped, extremely nimbly for a man of his girth, through the crowd. Colin saw him appear behind Christine and her new friend.

"Hey, Christine!" Shane shouted. He had a voice at least as expansive as his gut, and every head in the bar turned towards him.

Christine took her tongue out of the good-looking guy's mouth and sneered at Shane. "What?"

"It's herpes!" Shane shouted.

"What?" Christine asked again, her expression turning into a look of profound concern.

"That bump on my dick," Shane shouted, now the complete nexus of attention in the building. "You know, that bump that matches the one you have." Shane pointed towards Christine's recently grinding crotch. "Well, I had it tested and it's herpes. The doctor said there are pills we can take, but you have to go in and see him yourself. He wouldn't give your dose to me."

Everyone in the building gasped together, then laughter erupted.

The good-looking guy began wiping at his leg and fled through the crowd while Christine spun in a circle, a horrified expression on her face, as she saw the dozens of people laughing heartily at her expense.

"No!" she cried. "He's lying." She could barely be heard over the gales of hilarity, and Colin doubted anyone would believe her even if they could.

Shane, wearing a deeply satisfied smile, returned to the table, picked up the half-empty beer jug and gulped down the rest of it. "Let's get out of here." He set the jug down with a thump and tilted Colin a heavy wink. "I believe my work is done."

Now

"What are we doing here?" Fred asked, leaning forward to look up through the windshield of his pickup at the front of a run-down apartment complex.

"We're gonna ask some questions," Colin said, opening the passenger door.

Matthew leaned forward between the bucket seats. "I think this is a bad idea." He blinked up at the building. "Really bad."

"Matthew's not wrong," Fred said, placing a hand on Colin's arm. "I think we should leave this alone. It's not going to help."

Moving his arm from under Fred's hand, Colin shrugged. "I'm not going to do anything. I just want to talk to a couple of the neighbours, see if they noticed anything strange." Without waiting for further discussion, he slipped off the seat of the truck and slammed the door behind him. Five steps away from the big vehicle, he heard the other doors open.

"But you were here already," Fred said, as he hurried to catch up.

Colin said nothing for several steps. "I wasn't really thinking, then."

Tyner Gillies

The tenant listings at the front door of the complex had a buzzer number for the building manager, and Colin rang it. He had given back Shane's key when he went to tell Shane's mother that her son was dead. He should have hung on to it, but when he thought of how long it had been since he'd last talked to his friend, he didn't feel he deserved to have it.

When the call was answered by a gravelly, annoyed voice, Colin explained who they were and said they were there to pick up a few things from Shane's apartment for the family. Several minutes later, a hunched, leathery old man appeared and opened the door.

The man was below-average height, but the wild strands of white hair sticking straight off his liver-spotted scalp gave him the illusion of more height.

"What you say you wanted?" the manager asked, as he held open the door and let them into the lobby. He puffed busily on a wrinkled cigarette.

Colin glanced from the old man to the neon-green "no smoking" sign pasted by the front door. The man looked in the direction of Colin's gaze, grimaced, and blew a long plume of smoke into the air above Colin's head.

"We just wanted to get into Shane's apartment." Fred said. "Grab a couple of things for his family."

"Shane?" The manager took another drag on his battered cigarette. "That the fat guy?" Short jets of smoke shot out of the man's mouth, as he spoke.

Fred and Matthew waved their hands in front of their faces in a vain attempt to ward off the cloud.

"Yeah," Colin said, and took a deep, smoke infused breath to steady himself. His second last nerve gave way with a nearly audible ping. "Shane was the heavy guy. Died recently."

"Overdose." The manager took another drag.

"Yeah." Colin stuck his hands in the pockets of his slacks.

The manager shrugged and started walking down the hallway, pulling a ring of keys from the pocket of his dirty jeans. "You can go in there if you want. It stinks something awful, though, and the cleaning crew ain't due until Monday."

"Why does it stink?" Fred asked.

The manager stopped and turned, one eye squinted as

smoke from the cigarette stuck in the corner of his mouth drifted up around a sneer that was almost pleased. "Why does it stink? 'Cause the fat guy rotted in there for a week afore someone came and found him. He was getting pretty ripe, you know?"

Colin's final nerve snapped and he lifted his hand, reaching for the old man. Fred intercepted the hand and yanked it down before any harm was done.

"No, we didn't know," Fred said, his words clipped and brisk. "Thanks for telling us."

The manager shrugged again and turned down the hallway.

When the old man was a few steps away, Fred, still holding on to Colin's wrist, pulled him in close. "This was your idea, Colin." Fred's voice was a low, impatient growl, their faces were so close that Colin could feel stray hairs from Fred's beard tickling his chin. "This was your idea, so don't fuck it up now that we're here."

Fred was right, Colin knew, and he nodded. "Yeah. Okay."

Satisfied, Fred released him and turned after the old man. Matthew flanked Colin and placed a hand on his shoulder. Together, they followed Fred.

Shane's apartment was a short walk down the hallway, at the rear corner of the building.

"Here it is," the old man said, fitting a brass key into the lock and turning it. "The stink is too much for me, so I'm going back to my place. Buzz me when you're done and I'll lock the door." He withdrew the key and turned to leave, then stopped. "Oh, and anything you don't take now is going in the dumpster on Monday. Just so you know."

Colin opened his mouth to speak, but stopped when he felt Fred's broad hand squeeze his shoulder. He shut his mouth with a click and took a deep breath. "Okay. Thanks."

The old man slipped his key ring back into his pocket and turned down the hallway.

"Are you sure you want to do this?" Fred asked, as Colin reached towards the door knob.

"Yes," Colin lied. He didn't really want to do this, but felt compelled to. He looked at the door and realised it was the second time he'd ever been there. He knew the block of apartments because they'd been a fixture in town when he'd lived there, but he'd had to get Shane's mother to tell him the unit number. For however long Shane had lived in this place, struggling with whatever demons haunted him, Colin had never darkened his doorway. He hadn't called to see how Shane did. He hadn't even sent him a text message to say hello. After all the times Shane had come through for him, Colin hadn't even tried to come through for Shane.

Then

Colin glanced down at the hastily scrawled notes he'd made after the phone conversation he'd had with the Vancouver Police Department recruiter earlier in the day, and rubbed his hand across his forehead for the tenth time in the last two minutes. They'd had a recruit drop out of the training class that was set to start in the autumn at the Justice Institute and offered the spot to Colin, conditional on him attending a final suitability interview at the city headquarters tomorrow morning.

"So what are you going to do?" Fred asked, from the other side of Colin's parents battered kitchen table.

"I don't know." Colin rubbed his forehead again. "I don't think I can make it."

"How long will the flight take?"

"It's only forty-eight minutes. I could get on a flight tomorrow morning and make it in plenty of time for the interview, but the flight will be almost five-hundred bucks. I just don't have it." He'd asked his parents for a loan, but they were strapped even tighter than he was, and borrowing his old man's run-down truck was out of the question. Even if Colin's dad didn't need it for work, Colin didn't think the old beast could survive the journey.

"I wish I could help you, man," Fred said, rubbing at the short beard he'd been working on for a couple of weeks. "But I'm tapped, too."

Sitting back in his chair, Colin pressed the heels of his hands against his eyes. "I'm screwed."

A vigorous pounding at his door made him sit up bolt

straight. When he answered it, he saw Shane on the porch, Matthew behind him.

"Why are you just standing there looking ridiculous?" Shane asked. "Get your shit together."

"What shit?" Colin asked.

"The shit you need for your interview. We gotta get on the road."

"I don't think I'm going, man. I don't have any wheels."

Shane jerked his thumb towards the driveway in front of the house. "I talked my old man into letting me borrow his car. I've got two cases of Red-Bull and a bag of beef jerky. You sleep. We'll drive." He twirled his finger to indicate himself, Fred and Matthew. "We can all throw in for gas money and have change left over to get celebratory chicken nuggets when you ace this thing."

Colin could only stare, open mouthed.

Shane clapped his heavy hands together. "Come on man, this is important. It's your future we're talking about. If we're gonna make it, we gotta go."

Suppressing the urge to cry, Colin wrapped Shane in a brief, tight hug, then ran to get his thrift store suit and shaving kit.

Now

The inside of Shane's tiny apartment resembled nothing so much as a garbage dump, with special punctuation on the smell.

"Sweet Jesus," Matthew said, gripping his nose.

"How did he let it get this bad?" Fred asked, making no move to cover his face, wrinkling his nose.

Colin wanted to tell his friends that the smell was better now than the last time he was there, but he thought it better to keep that particular piece of information to himself.

"What are we looking for?" Fred asked, as he gripped his beard and peered down at the floor.

"Anything that will give us an indication what happened to Shane," Colin said.

Fred glanced up at him. "Don't we already know that?"

"Anything that will tell us *why* it happened, then."

Matthew went into the little kitchen, the sink brimming with brackish water, the counter covered with restaurant wrappers and bits of moldering food. Fred stalked, still holding his beard, into the living room. Colin, stepping over piles of trash, went into the bedroom.

The bedroom was much as he had last seen it. Only the air mattress, without the weight of Shane's cadaver, looked like a deflated party balloon. A heavy brown stain marred the surface, crusted at the edges, but still a little moist in the center. The awful smell that permeated the tiny dwelling originated from that brown stain. Colin had to summon all his will to keep from gagging.

A cheap dresser with ragged corners and a tilting nightstand were the only other furnishings in the room. The night stand was covered in small square bags and uncapped syringes. Colin bent down to examine the bags and saw the lightest dusting of blue powder in the corners.

"Fentanyl," he muttered. Vancouver's downtown east side was lousy with the stuff, killing users by the hundreds, but he hadn't suspected it would be this far north. He glanced over at the stained sheet on the air mattress. He also hadn't suspected that Shane would be using it.

He was bending to open the top drawer of the rickety dresser, when he heard a heavy, exhaled breath behind him. The sound was filled with regret and longing, close enough that he felt the breeze of it on the back of his neck. He turned. Nothing. He rubbed the back of his neck, where the hairs still stood on end, and glanced out into the short hallway. He was alone.

"Anything in there?" Fred called from the living room.

Casting another look around the room, making sure he was alone, Colin cleared his throat. "No, nothing,"

"This is weird," Matthew replied from the kitchen.

Colin stepped out of the bedroom, pulling the door closed behind him so none of his friends could see the stained sheet on the mattress. He shuffled through the garbage to stand behind Matthew in the tiny, filthy kitchen. "What did you find?"

"It looks like a pay stub," Matthew said, his voice nasally because he still held his nose. "But it doesn't have Shane's name on it."

41

His Cold Coffin

Taking the paper and looking at the name, Colin ground his teeth together so hard they creaked. "God dammit."

"What?" Fred asked.

Colin showed him the name.

"Tim Canyon?" Fred said, pulling his chin back so his beard spread across his chest. "The loser we went to high school with?"

"Yeah." Colin nodded. "He was Shane's dealer before his first stint in rehab." He crumpled the piece of paper. "This is a stub for a welfare cheque, and it's dated two days *after* the approximate date of Shane's death."

"What's that mean?" Matthew asked.

"It means Canyon was in this apartment after Shane died, and probably sold him the drugs that killed him."

Then

"I don't know, dude," Colin said, looking over Shane's shoulder at the new arrival to the party. They stood in the entrance to Fred's small kitchen, and Colin peered suspiciously into the living room. "I don't think you should be hanging out with him."

Shane turned and looked at Tim Canyon, who smiled easily and talked with several of the other people Fred had invited to his parents' tiny house for Colin's going away party. "Pfft." Shane waved a meaty hand in a dismissive gesture. "He's good shit. And he brought beer."

"Isn't he a bit of a burn out?" Colin asked. "I heard he sells a lot of weed."

"Dude, don't be ridiculous. I said, he *brought beer.*"

"You know where I'm going tomorrow, right?" Colin asked, his patience beginning to slip. Shane was well past the point of drunk, as he was so often lately. Since his dad had died of a heart attack six weeks before, Shane seemed to spend all his time drinking and arguing with his mother. Tonight, he'd killed at least half a case and was turning into a pain in the ass—which he usually did, drunk or sober.

"You're going to be a man of the law!" Shane shouted, as he

raised a full beer bottle. The other attendees of the party cheered around them. "And I'm damned proud of you, too." He began draining the bottle with noisy gulps.

Colin glanced around and gave a vague wave to his friends. "Do you think it's a good idea to have a drug dealer at a going away party for a guy who is on his way to a police academy?"

Shane lowered the bottle, now empty, and set it with a clunk on an end-table beside the ragged couch that took up most of the living room. "It's all good, man. I told you, he's good shit. And he brought *beer.*" He reached into his back pocket and produced another brown bottle, beads of condensation running down the neck. As he twisted the top off, he tilted Colin a wink, then called out a greeting to someone elsewhere in the house and was gone.

"What was that about?" Fred asked, as he stepped up beside Colin, a slice of three-for-one pizza in his hand.

Colin crossed his arms and let out a huffing breath. "Shane brought Tim Canyon to this little soiree."

"Is that a problem?" Fred asked. "You want me to give him the toss?"

"I don't like that Shane's rolling with him," Colin said. "I have a sinking feeling that it's going to turn out bad."

Now

"This is a really bad idea," Fred said, jogging down the dirty alley to keep up with Colin's furious stride.

Colin ignored him. A red mist had descended on his vision, taking him past the point of reason. Someone had to answer for Shane's death, and now he knew who it was.

After seeing Tim Canyon's welfare stub, Colin had left the apartment in a furious rush, and bullied Fred into driving from the residential area into the shady end of the down-town core; the place where you only visited after dark if you were up to no good.

"How do you even know he'll be here?" Matthew asked.

"For his sake," Fred said, "I hope he isn't."

Colin stopped, as the alley emptied into a narrow roadway

between old businesses. The dark sidewalks were mostly deserted, and he immediately picked out the person he was looking for. "You know what they say about old habits..." He turned to his right and walked briskly towards a lone figure standing at the edge of a circle of light cast by a street lamp.

A little thinner, a little rougher on the edges, Tim Canyon appeared much as Colin remembered him. He even stood on the same corner he'd used for selling weed in high school. He looked up from the bright screen of a smart-phone, when Colin was within a dozen steps of him.

"Hey, man," Tim said, pocketing the phone. "What you need?"

As Colin stepped into the pool of light, Tim's eyes widened. He opened his mouth to speak, then turned and tried to run. Colin took two big, quick, lunging steps and shoved Tim with both hands, sending him crashing into the brick wall behind him. The air went out of Tim with a little yelp and he slumped to the ground. Colin crouched over Tim and seized a handful of his filthy coat, pinning him down, as he cocked his right hand over his shoulder.

He knew he shouldn't, but Colin felt himself smiling.

Before he could smash his fist into Tim's lolling head, Fred caught up to him and hooked a big hand in the crook of Colin's elbow. Matthew grabbed Colin's other arm and tried in vain to haul him up.

"Colin, stop," Fred said.

"No," Colin said, his glare locked on Tim's face. "He killed Shane, and he's gonna pay for it."

"Please." Tim stared up at Colin, his face white with terror. "Please. I didn't know he was gonna take so much. I didn't mean to hurt him."

Fred leaned forward, his face next to Colin's. "Think about Shane," he said, his voice low.

"He wouldn't want you to do this," added Matthew.

Then

"Oh, Jesus," Colin said, taking a sip from his beer.

"What?" Fred asked from where he leaned against the railing of the front porch.

"It's her," Colin said, jerking his chin towards the street.

"Oh, Jesus," Fred said. He turned around, covering his face with his hand.

Clicking up the driveway in her high heels stalked Christine, a slim, pretty man following in her wake.

"What the fuck, Colin?" she yelled, as she got close enough to recognize him. "You were going to leave without even telling me?"

Matthew, deep in conversation with a pretty, spikey-haired blonde girl, turned to look, and then held up a questioning hand. "Is she serious?"

"You broke up with me six months ago, Christine." Colin turned for the door to the house. "I didn't feel like I owed you a goodbye."

"Don't you walk away from me," she ordered.

Colin ignored her and reached for the door handle.

"Hey, fuck face," Christine's companion yelled. "Get your ass down here and apologize for turning your back on the lady."

His hand above the door handle, Colin stopped, and turned to Fred. "You know, I would never hit her, but I could live with hitting him." He turned and put his hands on the railing to leap over, when something snagged his belt and pulled him back.

"Settle down, there, trigger," Shane said. He released his hold on Colin's belt and took a long pull from another beer. "What's going on?" He stood on his toes and looked over the top of Colin's head. "Oh, it's her again."

"I said get over here and apologize." The slender man pointed at the ground in front of him, as though he were addressing a naughty puppy.

"And she brought a friend," Shane said, his voice dropping dangerously, while his hand tightened audibly on the slick surface of the beer bottle.

"Don't you ignore me," the slender man said, stalking across the front lawn, Christine right behind him, to stand on the other side of the railing. "Get out here, now!"

Colin moved to leap the rail again, his temper flaring, but Shane stepped in front of him, blocking Colin with his bulk.

"It's time for you to go," he said, addressing Christine, but glaring at her companion.

"Fuck you, Shane," she said. "I'm not going anywhere."

Not taking his eyes off the pretty man, Shane pointed his finger at Christine. "You need to leave, now, or something terrible is going to happen."

She cocked one hip out and crossed her arms. "I said I'm not—"

Whatever she was going to say was cut off by a shriek, as Shane reached out with one meaty hand, grabbed hold of the pretty companion's shirt, yanked him bodily off the ground and head-butted him in the face.

Shocked, everyone stared at the fallen form of the slender man, except for Shane who noisily slurped his beer and the boy stringing shrill threats.

"I'm gonna call the police! I'll see you in jail!" he shrieked, as he clutched at his shattered and bleeding nose.

"Jesus, Shane," Colin said. "Why did you do that?"

Shane set his empty beer bottle down on the railing, and then took Colin's face in both his hands. He pulled Colin close, until their foreheads touched, and for a moment looked dead sober. "I did it because he was trying to hurt you. He was trying to hurt your future. You're the best of us, Colin, and you have a real chance to get out of here. I couldn't let him ruin it."

As suddenly as Shane's sobriety appeared, it fled when he snatched a beer from another party goer and drank deeply from it. "I love you, Colin," he said and walked back into the house.

"I love you, too," Colin said to his back.

Now

"What do you think, Colin?" Fred asked, his voice still low and even, as he squeezed Colin's upraised arm. "Is this what Shane would want for you?"

"Some things need doing," Colin said, not taking his eyes off the blubbering face of Tim Canyon. He yanked his arm free from Fred's grip, and cocked it back again, when he felt a breeze touch the side of his face and heard a single, whispered word in his ear.

"*No.*"

He snapped his head up, taking his eyes off Tim, and looked back at his friends. They intently watched him and gave no indication they'd spoken or heard anything.

Colin looked around, lowering his arm. Down the street, he saw a familiar bulky, broad-shouldered figure pass through the light of another street lamp. He narrowed his eyes and peered into the darkness beyond the distant circle of light. Nothing.

Letting his arm fall to his side, Colin shook his head. He glanced back at Fred and then down at Tim. "No. You're right. Shane would not want this." With a shove, he released Tim and stood up straight. "My friend is lying in his cold coffin and it's your fault. Can you live with that?"

Pulling his knees to his chest, Tim buried his face in hands. "I don't know."

"Figure out how," Colin said. "I've got a lot of things I have to learn to live with, but I won't live with this."

He turned from Tim's quivering form and was grateful when he felt Fred's heavy arm settle across his shoulders.

"This is the right thing," Fred said, while Matthew threw his arm over top of Fred's and fell into step beside them.

"It's a long way from right," Colin said. "But it's what Shane told me to do."

Memories of Miss Mindy Tulane

By Jen Frankel

This is the eye I see ghosts with," said Miss Mindy Tulane, war veteran and sometime librarian. She opened it wide, yellow-bright, but unseeing.

Terrified, the child across from her let out a cry. His sleeping mother jolted upright and slapped him.

A young porter outside the doorway stuck his head in and admonished her. "Madam, please," he said. "We'll have none of that."

The small boy took a deep breath and began to wail.

The woman, mortified, pulled the child by the arm from the compartment. The porter touched the brim of his cap and withdrew as well, leaving Miss Tulane alone.

Miss Tulane disapproved of corporal punishment. This little terror, however, had grabbed the letter she was reading right out of her hands. Snatching it back from him had ripped the paper.

Then he called her blind eye *weird*. The eye often made people look twice at her. To the children she read to in the Harlem branch of the New York Public Library, she was a sorceress, equal parts magical and terrifying. But never just *weird*.

Miss Tulane knew she should feel guilty that the child had been punished for something that was essentially her fault. But her thoughts had always run far deeper than her emotions and, truth be told, she rather appreciated having the compartment to herself.

To ensure it was still legible even if damaged, she unfolded the letter and read again:

> *Dear Miss Tulane,*
> *I admit that your letter has stirred some rather ambivalent feeling in me, returning me to a very difficult time in my life. Yes, I will show you the artifact, but no, I will not tell you any more until you arrive. There are more ghouls than genuine souls that visit me, and I must protect myself from opportunists.*
> *If that circumscription meets with your agreement, I shall expect you at your earliest convenience. Please bring the object you mentioned, as a show of good faith. Without it, I shall probably turn you away.*
> *Mr. A. Bagnall.*

Miss Tulane folded the letter and returned it to her purse. She took out the object which intrigued her correspondent, a small pin enamelled with the word *Halifax* in bright red. It was the only thing that Miss Tulane owned that mattered a jot, because she had no idea why she owned it at all. Why Halifax? Why a cheap trinket linking her to that place?

No, she decided. It didn't bother her that the child had been punished. He deserved to be, even if it was for the wrong thing. On the other hand, the lie she told him did trouble her. She placed a great deal of stock in honesty, because truth was something she struggled with daily. This fib was more straightforward than most she'd told. She did not see ghosts with her blind eye. That would have been foolish. She saw them with her good eye, the right.

Memories of Miss Mindy Tulane

After what she'd done in life, perhaps it would be more surprising if Miss Tulane did *not* see spirits. As she sat primly in her compartment, the train wending its way north through the Adirondacks, she thought of the boys she'd transported during the Great War. She'd been little more than a girl herself, driving an ambulance through the mud-rutted tracks of the French countryside. There had been horrors enough in those days. Why wouldn't she have seen ghosts?

She didn't recall the absolute first time she witnessed the phenomenon, because she'd never cared to. It sufficed that as long as she could remember, she had been able to see the spirits of those about to die.

It should have been terrifying, or at the very least unsettling. They appeared to be tethered to the bodies of those about to die, hovering translucent images of their originators. The spirits grew increasingly more solid, as death neared, their twisted faces giving every indication of great distress. They did not speak, but they clung to their dying selves, as some unseen force was pulling them backwards, away from the object of their desperate hope.

As death became final, she would see a look of comprehension, or at least of some terrible finality, enter the eldritch, glowing eyes, and—as if a thread tying them to their corpse had at last been severed—they would depart at what Miss Tulane thought of as "a fair clip," and vanish into the air.

Miss Tulane didn't lie about the ghosts, because she'd never told anyone about them. Not until that odious child, and look how badly that had gone. Her lies served a purpose: they kept others safe from the horrors she knew.

Customs officials boarded the train when it reached Canada. Miss Tulane tried to look less tense than she felt, but she passed scrutiny without a second look. Her current passport identified her as *Hildegard Restall, 46, of New York City, NY*. She had borrowed the name from the grave of a dead infant the first time she needed to travel after mustering out of the army.

Unable to afford a sleeper car for the Montreal—Halifax leg of the journey, Miss Tulane dozed in her seat, as erect in slumber as she was when awake. Initially, taking passage on a steamer to Halifax direct from New York had seemed like the most efficient way to travel, but there had been nothing sailing at an expedient time. Although she would never admit it, this was a relief because there was another secret she had kept through all these years.

Miss Tulane found her ghosts more pathetic than unnerving, but being at sea terrified her.

When her service in the military had required water crossings, she used sheer force of will to keep her phobia in check. The nights were the worst. Each and every one she spent aboard a ship, she confronted the same frightening images in her sleep.

The nightmare had a curiously peaceful beginning, a sense of slight claustrophobia, and darkness broken by hazy beams of light. She could hear the lonely tolling of a distant bell over the faint sound of a child singing "Beautiful Dreamer." The terror began when she started to fall. She plunged downwards, the descent slow but interminable. Death reached up for her from somewhere far beneath. To find peace, she needed to accept it, succumb to the end of her life. The longer she resisted, the more her fear grew, the greater her discomfort.

When Miss Tulane reached land again, the dreams stopped.

Aboard the train, she slept like the dead.

After three days in transit, Miss Tulane's nerves were raw. Not even mortar bombardments during the Great War had affected her so badly. Only her fear of water exceeded her current state. As the locomotive neared its terminus, Miss Tulane grew increasingly worried that her discomfort was obvious to those around her—a hellish thought!

As Miss Mindy Tulane inched toward the Canadian East coast, toward the sea, her stomach churned and her limbs became heavy. Unable to stay still, she paced up and down the train. The same young porter finally stopped her and asked if she was all right. Embarrassed, she retreated to her compartment.

Reaching Halifax, the porter offered his arm to help her down. She wondered if the young mother had explained the misunderstanding over the letter, or if the child had defended himself at all. What would any of them have thought if they knew Miss Tulane had only lied about the eye, not the ghosts?

Her temper was short and her mood foul when she departed her hotel the next morning. The nearness of the sea oppressed her. Every moment in this city seemed to erode her self-image of a woman who possessed unimpeachable equilibrium and resourcefulness. It didn't help that for the first time in years she'd had that dream, the one of drifting inexorably into darkness and death. She blamed the proximity of the Atlantic Ocean.

Although there were cabs in front of the building, she chose to walk, glad to delay her journey's end. She set out by foot.

Finally, Miss Tulane compared the return address on the letter with that of a small storefront off Barrington Street. Bracing herself, she went inside.

A bell tinkled as she entered, but no clerk emerged to meet her. Miss Tulane noted that the shop was devoted to the relics of nautical disasters, rather than more general antiques.

Miss Tulane ran a hand over a decayed board with the faded name of a ship, *The Lorelei*, painted in red, cracked and peeling. She shivered, imagining it resting at the bottom of the ocean.

A man cleared his throat, rousing Miss Tulane from her daydreaming.

"Good afternoon," he greeted her, a hint of England in his voice. "May I help you, Madam?"

"Miss," she corrected absently. "My name is Miss Miranda Tulane. I exchanged letters with you recently about an item that might connect me to my... ancestry."

"Yes, of course," he said.

He took her hand and pressed it with his own, surprising her. He looked ten years older than she, well-used by sun and salt water. She had seen the same hardened look on many naval men and civilian sailors alike, the same darkness in the eyes.

She took stock of how intently he stared into her eyes, both the good and the blind, and thought that he might be dangerous.

"This way," he said, and released her hand to lead her. "I am, as you rightly supposed, Arnold Bagnall."

She followed him with heavy steps. The air felt thick and difficult to breathe.

Miss Tulane was suddenly aware of a strange howling. She didn't need to look at Mr. Bagnall to know it existed entirely inside her own head. She thought immediately of the small icebergs in the mid-Atlantic that sailors called *growlers*. Air escaping from pockets inside them as they moved south sounded eerily like animals.

She heard something else, deep in her mind, along with the wail of the growler, a heart-stopping, dissonant groan of metal, scraping and rending.

Even more distressingly, she was unable to keep up with Mr. Bagnall although the shop was not large. When she reached the showroom in back, she halted.

Mr. Bagnall, realizing that the lady was no longer following him, asked, "Miss Tulane, are you all right?"

Slowly, Miss Tulane's amber eyes moved to his severe, lined face. Impulsively, she told the truth for the first time about what she saw with the good one. "I suppose not, Mr. Bagnall," she said. "You see, I am prone to visions of spirits from the afterlife, and one is standing at the end of this room."

Again, Miss Tulane avoided complete honesty. She did not mention that the ghost she saw beside the hulking cabinet at the end of the room was that of herself.

Although she had come to believe that ghosts were always tied to their own corporeal forms, this sight laid false all her notions. How could her own spectre be here when she was most certainly alive? How could it be hovering, its arm reaching into a case of pitiful treasures salvaged from a doomed ship? Most importantly, why had it taken Mindy's face upon itself?

Mr. Bagnall himself took her admission in stride. Could it be that he saw ghosts as well? He led her deeper into the room toward both the looming glass showcase framed in dark wood and the apparition. A carved plaque above the central doors featured the name of the most famous shipwreck of them all: HMS *Titanic*.

"It's the twenty-fifth anniversary of her sinking," Mr. Bagnall said. "When I received your letter, I found myself immediately transported back to 1919."

The year after the Great War ended.

"In that year, I finally mustered out and returned to Halifax," he continued, "half a man, changed almost too much to be recognized. Halifax had changed too. You know about the explosion of 1917?"

She knew, vaguely, of the carnage of that day and nodded. What a horrible time to be in this lovely town: the ghosts of the dead and dying would have been thick as fog. To have come from the devastation of Europe to a hometown changed so catastrophically? Traumatic as well.

"I lost friends and family that day," he continued. "Me, I worked as a wireless operator in the Great War. So the fate of Vince Coleman, the dispatcher who sacrificed himself for the safety of so many in that disaster, still haunts me. After the fire began in the harbour, he remained at his post, sending warning messages until the explosion took him.

"Do you know about the wireless operator on the *Titanic*? His determination was responsible for the rescue of what survivors there were. When I returned to Halifax, I began my collection of her artifacts, as a measure to heal myself. You may know that more than a hundred of her victims are buried here."

She nodded again, unsure of what to say.

"May I see it? As per the terms of our agreement," he asked.

Miss Tulane removed the *Halifax* pin from her purse and set it in his hand.

He examined it with a frown. "This I recognize: a tourist souvenir, distributed only in the early 1910s. I fear you have not been completely honest with me, Miss Tulane."

She had written to him of arriving for the first time in Halifax—or what she believed to be the first—in 1916 to travel to Europe with the Royal Canadian Army Medical Corps. Therefore, the pin would no longer have been in circulation.

She could make a case for it being a junk shop find, or a gift. Miss Tulane, feeling caught, straightened her suit jacket unnecessarily, and also her spine. Fingers of cold pressed along it and into the spare meat of her back. She had survived the most filthy and heinous of wars, and damn it all if a collection of antiques or its owner would defeat her.

With a deep sigh of frustration, Mr. Bagnall removed a small, wooden box from the display. He set it on a table between them. The ghost, lured along by some mystic urge, followed it and took up a position in the air above it. Miss Tulane tried to ignore the shade, but it kept drawing her the way the box drew it. A little chant began in her mind. *I am not dead, so it cannot be me.*

As she turned her attention to the box, a solution presented itself. A twin! A twin sister, dead at sea. That could answer the riddle of her phobia of ocean travel. Dead in Halifax? Dead in the explosion of 1917? But then, why would the apparition look like her as she was now? And how had it come to be here? A thought struck her: the child singing to her in her dream—could it be this woman, this possible sister?

Mr. Bagnall lifted the artifact's lid on creaking hinges. Now, she saw it was in fact a music box of a style not made since much earlier in the century. Patches of red felt clung to its interior. As the lid rose, so did a china ballerina, settling into place with a faint *twang* of its spring.

Terror surged in Miss Tulane.

Turning the key in the side of the box, Mr. Bagnall said, "The miracle is that the mechanism still works. It was salvaged in the early days after the tragedy from the wreck's flotsam."

"I thought the *Titanic*'s location had never been found," said Miss Tulane hoarsely. She wondered if she should beg him not to release the key.

"Rather, it was lost," he said, choosing to ignore her obvious discomfiture. "Fishermen knew at one point, at least the general area where it sank, but only a few were callous enough to take home what they found floating there. No, they did not dive to it," he continued, mistaking the hollow look in her eyes for a query. "By report, it must be below at least two miles of water. If it had settled on the Grand Banks, there would have been a chance, but it must be in the cold, deep water to the south. That's what the old-timers say, at least. But for a time, you could find debris floating on the surface in those parts: deck chairs and cases, umbrellas, other items. It must have been among those. As you can see, I've devoted much of my life to hunting down and collecting what others took from the site. But this child's plaything, it has brought me more pathos than the others combined. Maybe we both will solve a mystery today."

An even greater dread gripped Miss Tulane as Mr. Bagnall released the key, allowing the ballerina to begin her revolving dance. From the box itself emerged a series of plinks, as the cylinder inside turned. She recognized the tune immediately.

"'Beautiful Dreamer,'" she said, more horrified than before. "My favourite song."

After the mechanism ran down she asked, the words emerging in a whisper, "What connection does this have to me?"

He shut the box delicately as if it had not survived so much worse, and turned it over. On its base, a brass plate had been fastened. Despite some corrosion, it read clearly, "To my darling Abigale, from your adoring nanny Miss Miranda Tulane."

And then Miss Tulane did the inconceivable, and fainted.

She awoke on the carpet, thinking for a moment that she had chosen a terribly uncomfortable place for a nap.

Nearby, on a chair, Mr. Bagnall looked at her with dispassion. He had clearly left her where she had fallen. The apparition hovered over the table, focused as before on the music box.

"Well, Miss Tulane," he said, "I gather that you have been lying to me, and not just about your acquaintance with Halifax."

Inside, she felt a stirring of fear, as her life's foundation of lies crumbled before her one good eye. "Beautiful Dreamer" rang in her head as she sat up and forced herself to reply.

"Mr. Bagnall, my great secret, which I have kept not just from you, but from everyone, is that I have had no memory at all of my past before the Great War. Until now."

His eyes turned querulous, but he still made no move to

help her to her feet.

To her great embarrassment, Miss Mindy Tulane burst into tears.

"Abby," she said, remembering. "Brown ringlets and a hellion's temper, but sweet when it warranted. I suppose I took on my strength of resolve in response to hers. I gave her the music box the day we sailed. My own parents died when I was younger than she was then, leaving me in the care of the state. In those days, girls were ejected from the Orphan Asylum upon reaching the age of sixteen, and could expect no more to be done for us. I didn't mind. I wanted an adventure. I found a job with a family in New York and travelled there for the first time in 1911."

She looked up at the ghost, whom she now noticed had a blind eye too, the mirror of her own. Its pale face contorted in rage, as if angry at her for being alive. Still, it nodded, goading her to continue. "I had been with the family for such a little time. We travelled across the Atlantic in January by the south route, and were set to return aboard the *Titanic*. I failed them so terribly."

He kept his silence, forcing her to go on. "There was a little boy, too. Harold—Hally, Abby's brother. We sailed in second class, but their father knew many of the first-class passengers. His employer had bought our passages. He was the one who came to wake us when the ship began to founder."

The memories came fast now. The sound reverberating through the ship, through which the children had somehow slept. The sight of the ice, pink and blue in the starlight, passing outside the porthole window. Their mother's frenzy as she packed while Miss Tulane dressed the children, making a game of it. She was determined not show the children her own fear, so her body had tensed around it until it shrank into a hard ball of terror in the pit of her stomach. She had never been truly frightened again since that night. Truth be told, she had never felt much of anything.

The turmoil on the deck ran at a such a pitch that she felt unwilling to add to it. As for the children, she vowed to stand between them and the alarming truth. She placed herself there with conscious intent, even between them and their hysterical parents. The children would not see her terror, no matter what happened. The lies had begun that night.

Then, the rush of the water, its coldness. The way the children's hands were abruptly no longer in hers, how the screams of the people in the water around her were drowned out by the screams that seemed to emanate from the ship itself.

She saw her first ghost somewhere between the shock of the water and the moment she realised she was going to die. The green, unearthly lights of the great ship fell away beneath her, as if she instead had taken flight. Only the lights of the stars in the water showed the falseness of that illusion. The "unsinkable" monster of a ship had gone down into the water of the north Atlantic without a ripple. How could that be?

A piece of debris struck her in the left eye, and swelled it shut. The chill kept it from swelling more, and froze the blood in its tracks down her face.

Her life belt kept her head above the calm surface, but occluded her vision as well. She kicked, trying to turn herself in a circle to search for her employers and especially the children, but her feet were already going numb. In minutes, she could not feel them at all. Within half an hour, she could hear no more screams either.

But the ghosts, they were thick around her. They clung to the bodies of the dying, bobbing in their belts. They rose from the depths below long after the ship herself had vanished, its lights either extinguished or merely too deep in the black depths to see.

They brushed past her, travelling backwards into the night, their faces always turned toward their own lifeless bodies.

Miss Tulane hyperventilated in the cold, felt her tears freeze on her cheeks, and sang "Beautiful Dreamer." Long past all hope of rescue, a man's voice called out, "Anyone? Is anyone alive here?"

She found out later that her rescuer was the ship's fifth officer, a boy not much older than herself. Aboard the rescue ship, the *Carpathia*, she saw him once at a distance. As he went by, a woman's spirit departed backwards into the sky. The juxtaposition formed the illusion that he had drawn her ghost away with the force of his passage, but that was all it was: an illusion.

Her ghost was there though, chained by the past—or by

something stranger—to a gift she had given to a child who had died before eight years of age.

How was Miss Tulane alive? How could she have been apart all these years from her own spirit? Was this somehow the source of her notable courage and stability? Was her soul attached to Abby's music box as punishment for allowing that child to die so horrifically?

Only time would tell, she reasoned, if Miss Mindy Tulane reunited with her shade and continued on as a more complete person. If so, she would be glad of the years when she had not worried about the death and turmoil she had witnessed. Or, on the contrary, she'd discover that she had never left the doomed steamer at all, and at some unknown time, she would find herself flying backwards into the sky, away from a body that would again crumple to the floor of Mr. Bagnall's shop. Away from the music box that must, somehow, be her true corporeal form.

Her nightmare came to mind: *Darkness surrounded her. She felt terror, but also resignation. She was going to die. All that remained was to accept the fact.*

Arnold Bagnall stared at Miss Tulane as she travelled deep into her thoughts. Compassion came into his eyes as he recognized her as a fellow traveller through the worst life could offer. When he spoke, it seemed like a truth she should already have known. "I served as a wireless officer during the war, but on the *Titanic*, I was fifth officer, drawn to you by that song. When I pulled you from the freezing water, it was clear that you could never have been the one singing. Your skin was blue, and the blood from your eye had crusted around your lips. I have no idea how you were still alive. You were the last, the very last we rescued."

It seemed reasonable to Miss Tulane that the music box could never have found its way back to her except through someone also connected to that horrible event. They had the war in common too, and Halifax, the city to which the Carpathia had brought her...

"Mr. Bagnall," she said finally, as the last of the memories flooded from her, leaving only the sound of the music box repeating inside her head, "do you suppose this is all because I allowed those dear children to die?"

Memories of Miss Mindy Tulane

Instead of answering, he turned his gaze to the place where Miss Tulane's spirit hovered, clearly seeing it himself for the first time. His breath caught, and Miss Tulane wished she had the courage to reach out and comfort him. But all her strength was gone, lost in the past. She and Mr. Bagnall had been drawn together, against the odds. Could it be that there was a great meaning in their meeting again after all this time? She was certain that the apparition portended something greater, something not just about Miss Miranda Tulane and her years of shallow emotions and lies. The sound of that music box playing "Beautiful Dreamer" and the child singing along to it (was it dear Abby, or herself?) grew louder in her head, echoing in her ears and threading a pulse of blood to her useless left eye.

And then, with growing horror, she knew without a doubt, knew there was a shadow rearing up over not just this country, or North America, but the world. She relayed it in a shaking voice to the shop owner, speaking louder than she would have chosen, but needing to drown out the song:

"Mr. Bagnall, war is coming again. And this time, it will be worse."

Nowhere Time

By Pat Flewwelling

lia roused as the bus pulled into the terminal. She brushed the window's condensation away with her dirty, fingerless glove and leaned her forehead against the cold glass, wondering, *Why not here?* Her aching limbs vibrated with the lingering sensation of wheel rhythm. Some of the passengers disembarked to smoke in the dewy cold; the rest stayed aboard, drowsing. Nobody spoke.

From Peterborough to Oshawa to Sudbury, each town in Ontario had been the same. Every backstreet shelter in every town had its bullies and self-serving angels of mercy. She'd planned on going as far as Vancouver, but after twelve hours riding through hilly carpets of forest, she was sick of it.

Elia shouldered her ratty backpack and shuffled down the narrow aisle. If the bus left without her, it didn't matter. She needed air. As for wasting her fare, she could always bum spare change off the next load of passengers.

She stepped off the bus into wet, cedar-scented air that muffled sound. She could sleep in a place like this.

"I think you're on the wrong bus," a man mumbled. She

told him to mind his own business. She felt bad about it, though. From Sudbury to Blind River, the old dude had wept into his hands, only to fall asleep against Elia's shoulder. After the stop at Sault Ste. Marie, he'd prayed or meditated or whatever until they arrived at...wherever the hell they were now. She'd missed the sign as they were coming in.

A generation ago, the TransCanada Highway was as busy as a parade of ants, everybody driving their station wagons to roadside motels and quirky mom-and-pop gas stations. Now, nothing but caved-in tar paper roofs, weedy parking lots, and dirty people picking through bindweed, rubble, appliances, and old bicycle frames.

Sault Ste. Marie had been the worst. They had arrived at three in the morning along a stretch of industrial road, pulling in next door to a hotel. One wing had been stripped of curtains and furniture. A stuttering fluorescent light, swinging by one end, illuminated a colourless hallway of open doors. She knew the hotel was still in business because the hobbling desk clerk gave her the bum's rush when she tried to find a toilet and a vending machine. His eyes were so baggy his face needed a bra. There were eight sleepy, disgruntled people in the lobby waiting for him. Even the children looked like they'd had the colour drained out of them.

By contrast to the Sault, this unnamed little burg seemed downright inviting. Familiar, even. She recalled...what, happiness? Something to do with marbles and chalk.

She gave her head a shake. The gaps in her memory were filled with glue fumes, but she knew she'd never lived this far north as a kid.

Elia needed a stationary place out of the drizzle. There had to be a shelter somewhere in town. She memorized what she was leaving behind: a wide bulb-ended driveway with a dozen glass bus shelters, all modern and clean, and only the one bus. Fog fenced them in, with buzzing sodium lights casting everything in a sickly, yellow glow. People watched her go. One young woman began to follow, but she stopped at the last lamppost, reaching after Elia.

As far as Elia knew, this was just another town in flyover country, struggling to keep a four-digit population. It must have had greater ambitions of growth, once, because the road was four lanes wide, divided by overgrown islands. Patches of fog drifted in, thick enough to clutch in her hand.

Elia's world shrunk to a six-foot wide column; below her, the sidewalk was solid and real, sparkling with chips of quartz; above her, the clouds had frayed apart. It was a reflection of her whole life: nothing but the road under her feet, her few possessions on her back, and the dim sky to navigate by. The fog thinned, revealing a residential construction site. Half-built roofs rose above wooden slat fences that lined the street. Insulation wrappers flapped in the breeze.

Where there were houses, there was bound to be a gas station where she could ask for directions. She wondered if this was one of those weird urban planning projects that had no downtown core, which therefore made it harder for people like her to get by unnoticed. Still, she felt assured she was going in the right direction, and since the dull sky was darkening, she pressed on.

At all four corners of an intersection, there were more squares of fenced-in residences, the broad-beamed houses squatting shoulder to shoulder. She stopped at the red light, thinking, *Such big houses.* Were these people's lives so much bigger than anyone else's? They had no front or backyards. Did they spend their whole lives inside without ever seeing the sun? What did they do with so many rooms? Elia could have put her whole life in one of those upper storey rooms; a little kitchenette, a mattress on the floor, a closet to hang up her coat and hide her shoes away, and a dresser to unpack her clothes into a state of permanence. What could one nuclear family do with so much space? How could they afford to keep the place dry, warm, and in good repair?

Two blocks up, Elia recognized a break in the suburban formula. Other people headed that way, converging on that spot from all directions. Seemed like the place to be, so Elia decided to go that way, too.

She noticed the absence of road noise. No children playing. Not a park or a school in sight. She'd never seen a town so well designed to keep its noise down.

The light was still red in her direction. She laughed at herself for having waited so long. There wasn't a single car on the road, and no cops around to bitch about jaywalking. She began to cross.

A balmy, pillowy headwind pushed back, forcing her to hunker down and push through. Fatigue merged with tropical comfort, slowing her pace, weakening her resolve. She could have curled up on the crosswalk and purred herself to sleep, but itchy feet lured her on. She had to see what was up ahead. She knew this place, didn't she? Why else would her heart thump so?

The fences on this block weren't as solid. These wooden slats had collapsed inward, replaced in spots with rusted chain link and orange snow fencing. The houses looked like the kind built in a hurry during the 1940s and 1950s to keep up with the war effort and the baby boom, the kind with sloping porch steps and kitchens narrower than most bathrooms. She had stayed in a house like that in Peterborough, one with the bottle-dash stucco walls. She couldn't remember if that was one of her foster homes, or if an uncle had lived there, or if it was a friend's place. Tethered to the sandy yard was a red tricycle, strangled by wild grape vines. She'd had a trike just like that.

She had been here before. But where was *here*?

Houses gave way to vacant lots on one side of the street and a strip mall on the other. At the far, dead end of the road, there was a closed gas station with a single pump and a vintage logo. This was the large intestine of the city, with its service roads and working-man slums; on the other side of the mall, she was sure she'd find the clean people who wore well-coordinated clothes, had purses and keychains, and were always in a rush.

Elia had once suffered a lecture from an overly-cologned suit about how it was his duty to buy things even if he didn't need them, in order to keep hard-working people employed and off the streets. He claimed, therefore, that Elia had no right to beg him for change because he was doing enough already.

Elia laughed, because she'd forgotten all about him. Something about this neglected, brown brick, backside of the mall had reminded her of that combed-over capitalist. In fact, a store's sign, a papered-over door and a two-stair stoop looked like the spot she'd sat on, enduring the rich guy's rant. She even recognized the rock-and-concrete ashcan where he'd snubbed out his cigar.

Had she gotten herself turned around and ended up on a bus headed east along Highway 60? Missed Algonquin Park and landed back in Barry's Bay, or Kanata? Backtracked to Penetanguishene, where they'd locked up her father? Or Guelph, where the rehab centre kept a bed warm for her?

She squinted up at the sign. The glass logo had been busted in. That whole chain had gone out of business, what, ten years earlier? She pressed her hands against the filthy windows, peering between the tilted plywood boards. Empty display racks had tumbled in their frames. The floor was thick with ancient flakes of paper.

If this *was* the same place she remembered, then a huge grocery store and the rest of the strip mall would be connected by a wavy arch made of blue Plexiglas. Sure enough, mere steps to the left, she found the sheltered walkway.

Her hands rose at her sides, aching for...something. She stared at them as if they were possessed. What had she been holding? Someone else's hands? Someone on either side?

She remembered joy. They'd gone into a department store and bought a bag of discounted marbles, a yoyo, a box of coloured chalk, and a pack of soapy-tasting chewing gum. They had bought her a pack of lined paper, too, along with some thick, red-painted pencils that you find in kindergarten classes, and a couple of folders with pictures of kittens printed on them. She'd asked for a pack of scratch-and-sniff stickers, too. The wiry old man smiled and sadly told her no, because she really didn't need them. The fat old woman smiled, and once her husband's back was turned, she put two quarters in Elia's hand and told her to buy them for herself. Elia recalled with startling clarity the smell of strawberry-scented stickers and erasers that smelled like fake chocolate. Her heart swelled with the sense of the limitless possibilities of time and space and imagination.

Now she was back in this town, the name of which she could not remember. She touched the brick and recalled sitting in summer with her back against this very same wall, bracing papers against her knees and writing as fast as she could to keep up with the stories inspired by those empty folders and blank

Nowhere Time

pages.

And then what...?

She'd been alone for a while, but not forever. She'd been given the space and independence to dream, and then...

Grilled cheese sandwiches and warm tomato soup. After Saturday morning shopping, it was always time for lunch. She hated tomato soup, but she had those two lovebirds all to herself, and they loved her, and that was *their* time. They didn't talk much, but when they did, they always had something magical and wise to say. After soup and sandwiches, there were card games. Go Fish. Old Maid. When she was older; gin, canasta, and bridge. After games came hot chocolate, a bath, and a book in bed. She had a room of her own upstairs, with a window, a sloped ceiling, a nightstand, and a lamp with the shade still in its original plastic wrap. She had her own dresser too, with a mouldy, tilted mirror utterly festooned with nail-scraped stickers. The mattress was hard, the blankets scratchy, but everything always smelled clean and welcoming. Downstairs, the TV would be playing *Lawrence Welk*.

How could she have forgotten all of this? How could she forget their hometown?

All but the u-shape of the plaza had changed. Sluggish people went on about their business, wordlessly filing into stores she couldn't identify. She recognized only one of the shops, a two-storey department store across the cracked parking lot, with a wide, sloped overhang shading the picture windows. If she tried hard enough, she could remember which letters had fallen away. *S...man's* was all that remained of the neon sign. The windows were milky, and no one was parked out front. The double doors were wide open. She did know this place. That was the store where lined paper and off-brand Barbies came from. She pointed to it and turned to squeal glee at... at who? Her hands were empty. No one was walking with her.

But this place wasn't open for business. It looked condemned. The whole plaza, despite its seeming popularity, was structurally unsound. The potholed parking lot held only a handful of burned, abandoned cars; every store window was black and dusty; every sign dangled, painted over; sparrows flew in and out of eaves with bits of dry grass pinched in their beaks.

66

This was a dead place.

The whole city was dead.

Elia's heart began to thump. How could a whole town die?

Monochromatic people trudged across the asphalt in sporadic queues, each line disappearing into a different store. No one came out again. No one took note of her. They were figures in grey and white and black; she was wearing a bright blue jacket, and there was colour in her skin—surely they would notice her and come for her. Her hands seemed unnaturally vibrant.

Dread seeped into her heart. Something came out of the S...*man's* store. It had sensed her presence, and it was coming for her.

Despite her backpedalling, the distance between Elia and the S...*man's* store shrank, as if she was walking backwards on a forward-running travelator.

The S...*man's* store began to rumble. A wall on the left side shuddered, and the second storey thumped, as if it had fallen in its sleep. Dust erupted between the tectonic plates of its broken halves, billowing out towards her. The whole thing was coming down.

A man in a black suit came out of the S...*man's*. He looked like a ringmaster, top hat and all, and he was luring her inside with a wave of his arm. With another gesture, he drew out two people from within. They had white hair. One was short and lean. The other, saggy and round. They crept outside hand in hand.

"They're together again," Elia whispered. Her heart leapt with an ecstatic cry of despair.

Her grandparents. Reunited. So desperately loving of each other, and of her. Terrified of being torn apart ever again.

Elia clawed at her own chest, wailing, "They're together again!"

How long had death kept them apart?

Once her grandfather had died in body, her grandmother died in spirit. Grilled cheese sandwiches were no longer grilled. Tomato soup came from stolen ketchup packets and lukewarm tap water. The sheets began to smell like attic and dirty child.

They'd died so far apart, separated by county lines and a family's civil war over the assets. The family from Toronto and the family from Timmins squabbled over three acres and a two-bedroom house. In life, her grandparents had been the atomic bond keeping two volatile elements together. Once that bond was broken, Elia was thrown out at the leading edge of the fallout. She'd landed on her ass with her backpack in her lap and her face in her hands. Inside that pack was a bunch of bent folders, childish scribblings, and a crushed carton of chalk. After a month, the backpack was lost, and for the next eight years, she was rented out from one foster home to another, trading one garbage bag for the next until she aged out of the system. From then on, she had been a chronicler of place, grateful for any shared food, shared needle, or shared bed that came her way. No matter how old she got, she was a rootless child with arms too short to pull herself or her family together again. Year after year, she heard her grandparents wailing for each other. Their aching, her guilt, muted only by the liquid sleep Elia injected into the crook of her arm, the tracks marking time until the morning she didn't have to wake up.

"They're together again," Elia said, dropping to her knees.

Her grandparents looked horrified by their surroundings, horrified for Elia, and they clung together as if drowning in quicksand.

Hands caught Elia by the shoulders. "You don't belong here," said an urgent, feminine voice, hot against her clammy cheek.

The ringmaster offered his white-gloved hand to help Elia up.

"You don't *belong* here," the voice said again.

The *S…man's* collapsed on the right side.

"Look away," the young woman said, helping Elia stand and turning her away from the impending disaster. "Look away and *don't you forget* them."

"But I have to help them," Elia pleaded. "Everything's coming down!"

"If you don't see it happen, it won't happen. You have to leave this place. If you don't, they *will* be lost forever."

Elia planted her feet, twisting at the waist, but the other woman held her tight and blocked her view. Elia had seen this girl before, at the bus stop, frightened to see her striking off alone.

"This is the last place where souls go before they're forgotten forever," the young woman said. "You can't stay here. You don't belong here, because someone still remembers _you_."

Elia stared, uncomprehending. The girl was translucent and oyster grey, save for blue eyes, reddish freckles, and a lock of brown hair.

"Don't let them be lost forever," the woman said. "They're together now. You've seen them with your own eyes. It'll be okay now. You can still save them."

"How?"

"You have to share them," the woman whispered. "You have to make them live on in other people's memories. Only you can do it."

Grief rose up and crashed over Elia like a tidal wave, squeezing the air from her chest. She reached for anything solid—the young woman's shirt front—crushing it, screaming out all her horror and outrage and loss. She was losing them all over again, but how bittersweet to know at least they were together.

"Don't look back," the young woman whispered.

Elia obeyed, squeezing her eyes closed.

"Keep walking with me."

Elia felt the material of the woman's blouse in her hands. Her own fingers felt skeletal, iron-like, and sharp. They walked.

"Good. Hold onto them. Hold on."

A gentle hand smoothed her hair. The stranger's cold lips brushed Elia's ear.

"And when you go back, tell her Robbie-Jane says hello."

Anguish upsurged, crested, overwhelmed her. Elia wept as if it was the only way to restore life to her lungs. As if she was being born. And still the young woman pulled her along.

Back at the station, the other passengers mobbed her, expressing fear and relief, helping her walk the length of the bus on her wobbling legs, holding her up when strength failed and sobs drowned.

"It's time to go back," they told her. "Not our bus," they said. "Breathe." "Go back to sleep." "Hold on." They led her to a seat in the middle of the bus—a different bus, this one had soft orange cushions, not hard leathery purple seats—and they let go. On the seat beside Elia was a plastic-wrapped pack of lined paper.

The voices faded.

She was alone on the bus. The bus was moving. The vibration of the wheels was a comfort; the bus rocked her as she cried. She was back in the arms of the familiar, safe in transit, lulled by the sound of wind chimes.

Chimes became muffled metal.

The bus leaned hard, making Elia feel like she was rolling. She wasn't seated at all. She was lying down .

Slowly, she opened her eyes. Equipment was rocking where it hung beside her. She heard the sound of vinyl material, saw someone lean over her, smelled antiseptics and shampoo. A siren howled overhead.

The woman in the vinyl jacket gasped, and her eyes flared open with surprise and urgency. She wore thin blue gloves that almost seemed to glow in contrast to her dark sleeves. "Hey," she blurted, adjusting this thing and that. "You're doing great. Stay with me."

Elia recognized the voice, but not the face. Or was it the other way around?

"Do you know where you are?" She shone a pen-sized flashlight into Elia's left, then right, eye, before taking Elia's blood pressure and pulse.

Elia couldn't make sense of the things hanging from the open, metal cabinets, but she knew buses didn't have such storage. Where in God's name was she? Still in Ontario? Still in Canada? Her only geographical certainty was that she was back in the Land of the Living, because only there could her chest hurt so much or her throat burn so badly. Other than that, it didn't matter. She had another chance. This was her new Here, firm and unmoving.

"Can you hear me?" the brown-haired woman asked.

Elia couldn't respond. She couldn't move her tongue. It was being crushed to the bottom of her mouth, nearly gagging her.

"Just nod if you understand me."

Elia reached for the thing that was in her mouth, but her arms were too heavy to lift. The paramedic wiped Elia's lips and chin.

"Okay, I don't know if you can understand me, but you're on the way to the hospital right now. Won't be too much longer. We'll get you some—"

"Rah…" Elia croaked. Her mouth tasted foul, and she craved a barrel of water. "Robbie…Jane…"

The paramedic's green eyes widened and watered. Colour rose in patches and splotches, highlighting a spray of freckles across the bridge of her nose.

"Robbie…Jane…says…hello…"

Elia's eyelids were too leaden to keep open, but her fingers were working again. When she felt the paramedic's hand, she gave it a squeeze, transmitting all the gratitude and reassurance she could muster. She drew a shuddering sigh and willed her eyes open again. They were still in the ambulance, and the paramedic was crying.

They turned the corner.

Rebecca Raven

By David Tocher

ebecca Raven Wilson. To say Jason Stewart hadn't thought of her in a long time would be a lie. No, today was the day before the nine year anniversary of his sweetheart's death. Ever since then, he returned to his hometown on this date to see her family.

This year, to make the trip, he almost had to quit his new job at MacLeod Lumber in Prince George, British Columbia. He'd tried to swap shifts with a couple of co-workers. They turned him down in the usual manner: "I'm sorry. I wish I could, *but...*"

He had finally pleaded with his boss for time off, considered dropping to his knees. Did no one understand how much this meant to him?

His boss flatly refused. No surprise there. Dean Flynn, his supervisor—a tattooed, brawny fella from Thunder Bay, Ontario—specialized in three things: nattering nonstop about his sexual conquests, fistfights outside the bars along George Street, and running his crew at the lumberyard like a drill sergeant.

Dean had a favourite line he liked to use on his employees:

David Tocher

If you have a complaint, go write it on a piece of toilet paper and flush it down the shitter. He considered heartlessness a virtue and treated others accordingly.

Two days ago, before Jason decided to bite the bullet and tell Dean he quit, his co-worker Billy approached him saying he'd do the swap. Relief washed over Jason's heart as he thanked him profusely.

"If you need anything, you let me know," Jason had said.

Billy, a middle-aged man with blue eyes and greying hair, had shaken his head, smiling. "You pay it forward, brother. Next time you see someone you can help."

Now, behind the wheel of his orange-and-black '69 Charger, Jason travelled south along BC-97 toward Kensington, a city about an hour's drive from Prince George.

In the mid-September evening, the landscape raced past his windshield. Grass sloping to forest. Trees woven into fall patterns of gold, red, and fading green. Farmland dotted with cows and horses. Blue mountains rolling along the horizon. All these things flowed by as though an invisible river carried them in the opposite direction of his car.

Inside the vehicle, customized LED lights outlined the windshield, filling the interior with a green glow. A raven skull—arrow shaped, its beak's length curved to a point—hung from the rear-view mirror by a necklace of finely woven leather. In an aura of viridian candescence, it pendulummed gently, eye sockets blackly hollow, keeping watch.

A local news presenter droned on the radio. "The Kelowna Rockets beat the Prince George Spruce Kings two to one... Citizens are upset about how city funds are being appropriated...A man who lives on Kelly Road was taken into custody on suspicion of sex trafficking and murder...A power outage happened in 100 Mile House..."

As Jason turned the dial to a classic rock station, something on the shoulder of the road caught his eye. A blond-haired girl stood there, thumb out, wearing only a white hoodie and blue jeans. Her free arm was braced around herself, probably a feeble attempt to keep warm. He felt sorry for her, but he pushed it aside. The drive he made each year between Prince George and Kensington was *his* time, to be in solitude and remember

73

Rebecca. His ritual. He had no desire to share the trip with another soul.

Billy's words surfaced in his mind: *You pay it forward, brother. Next time you see someone you can help.*

Shit. The call to pay his debt had come early.

Jason pulled over.

Beneath the low, powerful rumble of his engine and his radio playing Joan Jett's "I Love Rock n' Roll" on 99.3 The Drive, he heard the girl's footsteps scuff-tapping against the blacktop as she scurried toward the car.

He unlocked the passenger door. She opened it, leaned in. Her one good eye and the other, swollen and black, scanned the inside of his car. Jason didn't blame her for exercising caution. She couldn't be a day over twenty. She'd clearly been assaulted, and here she was, smack dab in the middle of nowhere, jumping into a strange *man's* car. Risky business no matter the time of day.

After sizing him up, she offered her gratitude. "Thank you. I've been out here for hours."

"No problem. How far you headed?"

"Vancouver. But if I can get as far as Quesnel tonight, I'll be golden."

"Hop in. I'm going as far as Kensington."

Quesnel was thirty kilometres past Kensington on BC-97, the string of highway which ran north-south through the Cariboo.

Her eyes traced the interior again, this time lingering on the back seat to ensure no one else was hiding there. When she appeared satisfied that Jason wasn't driving a Rapemobile, she got in.

"What are you doing all alone out here like this?" he asked.

"Long story."

"Long story? Sounds, or rather, looks like a bad one too."

"*Believe* me. It is."

"Oh, I believe you. How's that eye of yours?"

She smiled thinly. "I guess you're not gonna buy the ol' *I-fell -down-the-stairs* excuse, are you?"

"Nope. But you don't have to explain. If you're okay, that's what matters."

Jason studied her to determine if she would give him any trouble or not. He considered the slight tremor in her voice and how she kept her legs together, her shoulders slumped, and her hands clasped on her lap.

This girl wants to be as inconspicuous as possible, Jason thought. *Hell, she'd turn herself into a ghost if she could.*

Jason had picked up hitchhikers in the past—all men—and before he'd pull away from the curb, he'd tell them his rule: if they wanted to ride with him, they couldn't wear a seat belt. Then he'd warn them that if they started a ruckus, he'd slam hard on the breaks and let them hit their faces on the dash, even go through the windshield if that's how it played out.

Looking at the girl, however, he felt another pang of sympathy, stronger this time now that he'd seen her black eye. She seemed harmless, and he decided not to enforce his seat belt rule. Jason put the Charger in first, pulled onto the highway, and geared up to a buck twenty.

"My name's Jason, by the way." He started to reach out to shake her hand, then thought better of it. After being assaulted, physical contact with a strange man was an unlikely desire.

She fastened her seat belt. "I'm Morgan."

The way she stuttered her name made Jason think she had lied. He could accept that. She was a young girl trying to stay safe out on the road. Who could blame her? He amused himself by   secretly nicknaming her *Maybe-Morgan.*

She leaned toward the raven skull swinging gently from the rear-view mirror, enrobed in shadows and green light, and reached out a finger to touch it.

"You like it?"

"It's beautiful," she said. "Where'd you get it?"

Jason gave her the side-eye, grinning. "Oh, that's a long story, too."

"Long story good or long story bad, like mine?"

"A little bit of both."

"You wanna tell it?"

"Sure. If you have the time."

She laughed lightly. "It's not like I have anything to do for the next while. I'm game for a story if you are."

Maybe-Morgan had a companionable humour in her voice. Nice. That meant she felt more comfortable now.

"Okay." Jason nodded at the raven skull. "I bought that as a one year anniversary gift for my girlfriend back in high school. It was in '09. I was seventeen."

Maybe-Morgan returned the side-eye and the grin. "Is that the good part or the bad part?"

"The good part. She died later that night."

Maybe-Morgan stayed silent a few seconds before she spoke.

"What was her name?" she asked.

Instant respect.

Instead of offering some bogus words of sympathy like most people did, she'd asked *her name*. The standard go-to for the average person was *"I'm sorry,"* or *"I understand."* Even though Jason was too polite to say anything, he would feel contempt for them. People weren't sorry and they *didn't* understand. They only said those things to alleviate their own discomfort.

"Her name was Rebecca Raven Wilson."

Maybe-Morgan smiled. "It's a beautiful name."

"Rebecca was pure Native. She was Waknakin Indian and she lived with her folks out on the reserve, north of Kensington. When we first started dating, she told me about her nation's raven legend."

Maybe-Morgan cut in. "I've been through Kensington a couple of times. You can see the band office from the highway before the bridge."

"That's right. There's the big raven mural on the side of the building that faces the highway. That's Waknakin.

"Anyway, she told me about how her mother gave her the middle name Raven as a tribute to this bird. In their tribe, each family member is honoured with carrying a token of this animal since they believe in the legend.

"Waknakin is supposed to be a giant Raven that can transform into a human at will, and all through their generations, it protects their families.

"When I was seventeen, I bought that necklace for her as a one year anniversary present. My plan was to take her out to dinner at her favourite spot—Diner on Delray, that little 1950s retro joint in North Kensington."

"I know that place. I ate there a few times as a kid. Isn't that in Watford though?"

"There was a vote back in 2010 and Watford became part of Kensington. It's no longer a separate municipality."

"I had cousins who used to live there. They had a house on Brown Street. We'd always joke about how—"

Jason and Maybe-Morgan finished the sentence together, laughing. "—Brown intersects with Butt Street. *Brown Butt*."

Their laughter tapered off and Jason continued.

"As things turned out, she and I were in a car accident that night. I survived. My girlfriend, Rebecca, on the other hand, wasn't lucky…"

Mid-September of 2009. In the Cariboo region, snow had fallen early, transforming the four lane blacktop into a winding stream of ice and mud.

Jason wanted to surprise Rebecca. He had prepared their night by purchasing a raven-skull pendant on a necklace of brown finely braided leather. Also, because he worked part-time as a dishwasher for Diner On Delray, he had asked his boss to keep the kitchen running after closing time to let Jason and Rebecca have a private party for two. His boss, a family friend, said he was happy to help.

Jason wanted to show Rebecca a special time. A night of dancing on the white-and-red-checked floor while '50s tunes played on the vintage juke. They'd enjoy their favourite meals and deserts on the menu and receive personal catering from Andy Bailey and his wife, Vivian, the owners. Jason had even arranged to have two menu covers modified to say, "*DINER ON DELRAY CELEBRATES JASON AND REBECCA'S ONE-YEAR ANNIVERSARY!*" complete with a picture of them together.

He parked his '83 Dodge Aries outside the Starbucks on the intersection of Water Street and Jasper Avenue, downtown Kensington's main drag, and waited for Rebecca to finish her shift.

Wearing her winter coat over top her barista uniform, she waved at him as she pushed open the front glass door and stepped onto the sidewalk. She stopped to stare up at the falling snow, then looked at him with her nose wrinkled in distaste.

This weather sucks, that look said.

He shrugged in reply.

Once she was inside the car, her big purse on her lap, Jason said, "One year now, Rave." He held a small box wrapped in green paper. Her favourite colour.

She leaned away and looked at him as if he was a complete weirdo.

"That's lame," she said.

"Excuse me?"

"You're the kind of guy who remembers anniversaries and you expect me to think you're a man?"

"You're kidding, right?"

"Do I look like I'm kidding?"

"I've been planning all week for this."

"Don't put this on me. I never asked you to."

"I looked everywhere to find the perfect gift for you and this is how I get treated? You know what? Screw this." Jason tossed the box on the dash.

"Oh, please," Rebecca said. "Wannabe tough guy acting like a big baby all of a sudden."

"Just go. Call your dad for a ride home."

"No." She reached into her purse.

"I really don't need this right now, Rave."

Rebecca withdrew a sealed envelope from her purse. "I'll tell you what you need. How 'bout you chill out and learn to take a joke? I'm only messing with ya."

She handed him his gift.

He smiled. "Oh no. You got me again."

"I love you, Jason. And the reason I love you is because I'm as lame as you. Happy anniversary."

They laughed together.

"A card, huh?" Jason said. "Wow. Big spender."

He tore the envelope open with his finger and removed the card. Inside it, he found a receipt for a $500 payment to

Mauro's Auto Salvage, a lot off the highway near Watford. For the past month, Jason had been eyeing the '69 Charger in that lot. It needed repairs, and Jason felt confident he could make them.

He had discovered his love for vehicles when he'd met Rebecca's dad, George, who had his own auto-repair garage on his acreage.

Shortly after Jason and Rebecca started dating, he had visited her parents' place, only to learn of George's Rule: if any boy steps onto his property to visit his daughter, that kid would be put to work. It kept them away. Once George coerced them into sweeping his garage, handing him tools, or helping him lug heavy car parts, they would run away from there the moment they had a chance.

Not Jason. When he met George—who at first eyed him coldly—he found himself handing the man tools and fetching him parts while George worked underneath a truck. Jason grew curious about everything, asking the man questions about mechanics. Next thing he knew, George offered him weekend work for ten bucks an hour, and began teaching Jason everything he knew.

"Rebecca," Jason said, "how were you able to pay for this?"

Her silence answered his question. She had been saving up her meagre wages at Starbucks so she could afford a trip to Manitoba. She wanted to visit her grandfather there once she graduated high school.

Jason shook his head. "This is awesome. Really. But I'm not sure if I can accept this. I know how much you wanna go to Manitoba."

"But you *can* accept it," she said. "And you will. Then, when you get your car all fixed up and street legal, you're taking me on a road trip. Deal?"

Jason nodded. "Deal. Now open up yours."

Rebecca unwrapped her gift to reveal the raven skull pendant inside the box.

"It's gorgeous," she said. Her finger traced the raven skull's outline, then ran gently up and down the finely woven braids of the leather necklace.

As he watched her, an involuntary wave of tenderness

flowed over his heart. Rebecca, a beautiful young woman with long black hair and dark eyes, had a figure that turned the heads of every guy and inspired the envy of every girl, but Jason cherished her for more than that. He delighted in the curve of her nose, the way she smiled, how she bit her bottom lip while concentrating. He adored how her hands flew everywhere when she talked in circles about something that fascinated her. In short, Jason had it bad. He loved her for all the intangible traits that made Rebecca distinctly Rebecca.

"It's gorgeous," she said again.

"Here, let me help you." Jason took the necklace gently from her hands and put it on over her head. When the raven skull was resting on her chest, he leaned forward and they kissed. Long, slowly, and softly.

"I'd love to do that all night," he said, keying the ignition, "but I've made plans for us."

Once they had crossed Lake Waknakin over the Charles Turgeon Bridge, they followed BC-97 north toward Watford. Rebecca took a pastry bag from her purse and began munching on a bagel.

"Seriously?" Jason said. "I'm taking you someplace special for dinner and you're gonna ruin your appetite?"

"My shift was crazy. I'm starving. I'm tiding myself over is all."

"Sorry, my bad. Don't let me stop you from pigging out. After all, it's what you do best, isn't it?"

Rebecca crossed her eyes and contorted her face at him.

Lined with billboards, the highway curved up a hill. Jason drove confidently and carefully. He had taken Rebecca 4x4ing in his dad's Dodge Ram in worse conditions than this.

When they crested the hill, the ambers were flashing. Jason braked for the red light at the intersection of BC-97 and Horizon Road. His car fishtailed gently on a patch of black ice. He would have come to a complete stop, too, if it wasn't for the driver behind him. He hit Jason's bumper with a loud *thuck*, pushing Jason's K-car into the middle of the four-way.

An eighteen-wheeler struck the driver's side door, crumpling it inward. Glass shattered. The car spun in circles and the world blurred into white streaks and lines of light. His junker toppled into the ditch and landed on its side.

The last thing Jason remembered before falling unconscious were Rebecca's eyes bulging and the *cuh-cuh-cuh* sound she made, choking to death on a piece of bagel.

"…I was all busted up in that accident. Wound up in the hospital for months. Rebecca? A bruise on her forehead. That was it. If she hadn't been eating that bagel, she would've lived."

He remembered her bulging eyes, her hands clutching at her throat, the choking sounds. The old panic and helplessness resurfaced. Nothing he couldn't handle though. After nine years of practice, Jason knew how to fight back against his mind's irrational urge to relive the horror.

"I'm never gonna eat in a vehicle again," Maybe-Morgan said.

Her candour caught him off guard. He burst out laughing.

"I like your style," he said.

"I lost my mom when I was a kid. It was rough. I get it."

Jason's respect for her grew. Even though he barely knew her, he did perceive one thing. Like him, she was separated from most people—part of a secret club with all sorts of its own unspoken rules. The thing that set her apart was that she had suffered great loss. A person from whom life chose to take rather than give. Meeting a fellow traveller such as her felt like talking to a stranger, only to discover that both of you shared a mutual friend.

Jason changed the subject. "What are your plans when you get to Vancouver?"

"What do you mean?"

"Didn't you tell me earlier that you were on your way to Van?"

"Right," she said. "Sorry, I'm tired. Vancouver, yes. You like it there?"

She had sidestepped his question by asking her own. Jason understood then that he had caught her in Lie #2. Not only did she wish to keep her name a secret, but her destination as well.

All things considered though, he gave her a pass. A woman with a black eye, hitchhiking alone, had every right to her privacy. If she didn't want him to know where she was headed—hell, maybe she didn't know yet either—then it was none of his business. All he needed to concern himself with was paying it forward.

"You hungry?" Jason asked.

"Oh, I'm straight-up broke," Maybe-Morgan replied.

"That's not what I asked you."

"Seriously. You don't have to buy me anything." A hardness in her voice now. Scared-girl-riding-with-a-stranger syndrome. If he insisted, she might feel threatened. Maybe another guy helped her once and tried to use it as leverage to make her do *stuff* for him. Scumbags like that filled the world. The girl could also be hanging on to her pride, refusing to be a charity case.

How could he make her feel comfortable with accepting his help? As he thought it over, Maybe-Morgan's belly groaned. He looked at her and saw the embarrassment on her face as she suppressed her laughter.

He smiled. "Do I have to listen to that for the rest of the drive?"

Her belly made more noise. This time a drawn-out groan that ended in a burbling snarl.

"Geez, Morgan. I'm scared now. You sure an alien isn't gonna come bursting out? Should I send for Sigourney Weaver?"

She couldn't restrain her laughter anymore.

The sound of it made him happy.

"Look," he said. "There's a restaurant up the highway. Black Pine Lodge. I'll stop there and buy you dinner before that belly of yours starts the alien apocalypse. You'd be doing me a favour."

"Oh, what the hell. Okay. Thank you."

Loverboy's song "Working for the Weekend" played on the radio. As Mike Reno chanted on about how everybody's lookin' to see if it was you, a lull settled in the conversation.

Maybe-Morgan yawned, leaning her head against the passenger window. "Thank you for being nice to me. No one has ever done anything nice for me before."

Jason was about to respond, but she closed her eyes and went sleep.

He hurt for her. What kind of world was this when a scared, hungry, beaten person felt the need to say thank you because someone had treated her with kindness for the first time?

The raven skull swayed gently back and forth, shifting in the shadows. It seemed to be looking from Jason to Maybe-Morgan, observing them, contemplating whatever raven skulls contemplate.

The Charger roared south, and Jason remembered.

A week after the accident, Rebecca's parents, George and Jackie Williams, came to see him at the Kensington General Hospital, where he was confined to a bed with his arm in a cast, leg in a sling, and his body covered in bruises. They would have come earlier, they'd told him, but the doctor wouldn't allow visitors. Besides, it wouldn't have done any good. Jason had been unconscious.

He expected them to hate his guts now, to accuse him of killing their daughter. Hell, he hated himself. Even though he knew it wasn't his fault—it had been that idiot driving behind him—that didn't stop the Molotov cocktail of guilt from exploding in his heart.

Jason tried to say something to them. He couldn't.

George must have known Jason's thoughts because he spoke firmly. "We're not angry at you."

Jackie caressed the side of Jason's face. "We love you very much. We know you took care of our girl."

Their words didn't take Jason's sadness away, but they did lift a huge weight off his shoulders, and made the situation a little easier to deal with. A *little*.

"George and I had the same dream," Jackie told him, reaching into her purse. "Rebecca told us to give you this."

She withdrew the necklace that Jason had given Rebecca the night of the accident. Up until now, Jason hadn't cried over Rebecca. Instead, his grief had been a dry well in his heart. At her parents' words and the sight of the raven skull, his tears flowed.

Jackie put the necklace on Jason. George asked him to listen carefully. He put his right hand on Jason's good shoulder, then told Jason to put his hand on George's right shoulder. Their arms crossed and formed a kind of X.

George recited something in the Waknakin tongue.

"What I spoke to you," George said, "is only allowed to be spoken by an Elder. What it means is this: As your arm and our arm cross, as the Fraser River and Chilcotin River cross, and as the spirit world and material world cross, your blood and our blood cross.

"This, my friend, is how an Elder welcomes an outsider into the tribe.

"In the Waknakin tongue, there is no word for *I*. If someone wants to say 'I'm hungry,' they can't. They can only say 'We are hungry.' This means that if one member of the tribe needs food, then everyone else does, too. By feeding that one person, everyone is feeding themselves. And a woman doesn't say 'my baby.' It's 'our baby,' meaning that the entire tribe helps the mother care for the child. That's why I said 'our arm' and 'our blood.' My arm is the arm of the entire tribe. My blood is the blood of the entire tribe."

Before that meeting with her parents, Jason would lie in the darkness, teeth clenched against the headaches, as he waited for the painkillers to kick in. He would whisper Rebecca's name and look out the window to where moonlight glowed behind barren trees. Empty silence, the only reply, withered his heart.

After George and Jackie's visit, though, Jason would hold the necklace in his good hand, drifting to sleep each night in solace, and feel Rebecca's presence in the room. Often, when he awoke, he wondered if he had imagined it all. Finally, he chose to think of it as the echo of her existence resounding in his heart—*life* waves, rather than sound waves, reflecting back on him.

In a time such as this, even an echo was enough.

Jason parked in front of Black Pine Lodge, a log building at the back of a gravel lot. Forest enclosed the property on three sides. Maybe-Morgan, still conked out, had her head resting against the passenger window. He shook her shoulder gently.

"Hey, Morgan. Time to wake up."

No answer.

He patted her arm this time. "Morgan?"

Still no response. Not even a sleepy mumble. Well, damn. When she said she needed some rest, that girl told no lies.

He leaned toward her and saw her one opened eye, staring blankly through the glass. He put his fingers to her neck—like his phys-ed teacher had taught him back in the day—and felt for a pulse. Nothing. Dismay rose up in him. *Relax. She's fine.* He turned her chin slowly, and when he could get a good look at her face, the truth of the situation sank in. She *wasn't* fine. She was dead.

Jason's own pulse boomed in his throat.

His hand wanted to retract as if from a hot stove element, but he resisted. He forced himself to set her head back gently against the window, then he pressed his fingers to her neck again. Nada. He calmly withdrew his hand and placed it on his lap.

He suppressed his panic, his body trembling.

His stomach sank; the same feeling as going down in an elevator too fast. He sat there, staring at the dead young girl, as a withering sadness seeped into his heart. Then a numbing sense of detachment came over him, an oddly comforting chill. He began to wonder if he'd float away out of his body.

He stepped outside of the car, took his first breath of crisp evening air, and that's when Jason began to fade out of consciousness. He told himself he couldn't faint. Not here. Not with the girl in the car like that. The grey-out passed. The world solidified in front of him again.

He removed his iPhone from his jeans pocket. His hands began to shake, and he dropped his cell before he could dial 911. When he knelt to pick it up, all the old panic and helplessness rose up, and this time he couldn't stop it.

He remembered Maybe-Morgan's dead eye staring blankly, the light from the restaurant windows reflected in her iris. This blended together with the memory of Rebecca clutching her throat, the *cuh-cuh-cuh* of choking on a piece of bagel, and the look of panicked dismay on her face. The pain in his head. The feeling of warm blood seeping into his jeans. The terror. The helplessness. He saw and felt everything in his mind's eye as if it were happening right now.

The tears flowed, and he roared through them.

"Sir, are you okay?" asked a waitresses standing outside on her smoke break.

"We need someone out here who knows first aid," he said, rising to his feet. "I picked up this girl hitchhiking. I was only trying to help. I think… think she's dead."

"Oh dear," the waitress said. "Not another one."

Jason looked at her, horrified. "What?"

"Never you mind. Call 911." She walked back inside the restaurant.

Onlookers gathered around. He opened the lock screen on his phone and punched in the appropriate digits.

After a couple of ring-back tones, a man's voice answered. "911. What is your emergency?"

The waitress brought one of the cooks outside. He checked the girl's pulse, confirmed that she was dead.

"Tammy, order this guy dinner on the house if he wants it," the cook said to the waitress, then looked at Jason. "You're white as a sheet, buddy. Go with Tammy. We'll wait out here 'til the police arrive."

"I hope you all understand I only wanted to help her." Jason instantly scolded himself for making explanations that nobody asked for.

Tammy, the waitress, put both hands on Jason's shoulders. "Nobody thinks you did anything, hon. You're not the first person to show up here with a battered girl he picked up hitch-hiking. Come on, now. I'll explain everything inside."

She seated him at a table near the fieldstone hearth where a fire crackled behind a mesh curtain. Tammy offered a bed in one of the back rooms if he needed, but Jason insisted he was okay. She brought him a burger and fries on the house. Jason devoured it.

"This area has a problem with sex trafficking," she explained. "A girl shows up for a fake job interview or goes to a party and meets the wrong people. Next thing she knows, she's kidnapped and forced into prostitution.

"Around here, there's what's called an exit fee. If a girl wants out, she has to pay a certain amount of money. Then her pimp beats the living shit out of her and leaves her out on the highway. It's always the same. A single black eye. But under the clothes? Beaten black and blue. Now, this girl probably had internal bleeding and didn't even know it. She was already dying when you picked her up."

Jason remembered how Maybe-Morgan had hugged herself on the highway's shoulder. He had thought she was shielding herself from the cold, but no. Also, her careful movements while she sat beside him. She wasn't shy or trying to make herself smaller. She was hemorrhaging to death. His heart sank with grief for her. He remembered the last words she'd spoken to him before falling asleep. *Thank you for being nice to me. No one has ever done anything nice for me before.* His throat constricted and his eyes began to fill.

"Exit fee," Jason whispered, feeling the shape of those horrific words in his mind.

Tammy pressed her lips together and frowned. "Other people have shown up here before. Sometimes the girls freak out if you let them know you've called the cops or the hospital. They've been brainwashed into being afraid of them.

"Ben, our chef out there, he brought in a couple of girls before. They caused a scene when he told them he'd call an ambulance. He's our first aid on staff. So now, if he's driving to work and sees a girl, he just drives past and calls the police to let them know where to find her. Then they can get her help."

Blue and red lights whirled outside. Jason looked past Tammy at the lot through the wall-length window. An ambulance and a police cruiser.

Two police officers. One was a musclebound giant over six feet tall. The other, a short guy, also jacked. They probably worked out together and called each other *Bruh.* Jason secretly amused himself and nicknamed them *Big-Dog* and *Short-Round.*

Big-Dog asked a bunch of questions, took witness statements, and gave out business cards. Short-Round checked the body and the inside of the Charger. They told Jason that if the police needed to know more, they'd call. According to the coroner's on-site examination, the girl had died of internal bleeding. Blunt force trauma. The attendants strapped the bagged body onto a stretcher and wheeled her into the back of the ambulance.

An hour later, it was all over.

After the police and the paramedics left, Tammy invited Jason to sleep on her couch overnight. "You're shaken up, hon. Driving alone at night in your state isn't such a good idea."

Jason politely declined.

He climbed in his orange-and-black '69 Charger and drove south along BC-97 toward Kensington.

The drive he made between Prince George and Kensington was his ritual, a time to be in solitude and remember Rebecca.

Tonight, however, he wasn't alone. Rebecca sat beside him in the passenger seat. Her flesh, once soft and brown, was now corpse grey and dotted with dark splotches. A white film coated her eyes. She wore a tasselled buckskin dress with red-and-black beadwork, the garment she had been buried in. Shadows and green light bathed her features.

Maybe-Morgan was there too, curled in Rebecca's lap.

Rebecca embraced her and, with her skeletal hand, caressed the girl's hair.

You're safe with me now, Rebecca told her. *Nobody will be able to hurt you anymore.* When she spoke, the radio crackled with static and the dashboard lights flickered.

As the spirit world and material world cross, your blood and our blood cross, Jason thought, and shivered.

Ahead, the lights of North Kensington arrayed the darkness.

AUTHOR'S NOTE

I would like to thank Chief Simmons of the Waknakin First Nation Council for generously teaching me Waknakin history and legends. In this story, I have done my best to follow his direction to ensure I wrote about their legends in a manner that respects their culture.

Relentless

By Repo Kempt

T he killing of the *tuktu* proved both a blessing and a curse. Its cherished meat would feed many starving Inuit families and the pelt would provide cash for both Mikkigak and Taukie. But the animal had cost the men precious time.

Rather than head for home, Mikkigak decided to shoot the caribou. Rising wind meant this choice had been foolish. Neither hunter wanted to waste time arguing with a blizzard bearing down upon them. Instead, Taukie mumbled a prayer while he secured the dead animal to the wooden qamutiik with ropes and bungee cords. Beneath his winter boots, the dried and frozen blood of the caribou appeared black against the stark white snow.

There was no time to do things properly. The storm had strengthened during their struggle to load the creature's body onto the already overburdened sled. The mountains to the east had all but disappeared from view, increasing cloud cover and swirling snow smothering the last of the faint sunlight. The men's arms hung heavy; their legs, languid. Mikkigak felt as if his blood had frozen to slush in his veins. They exchanged a final glance, one of urgency, then jumped on their respective snowmobiles.

"I'd told you we'd finish before it hit," shouted Mikkigak in Inuktitut over the howling wind, his long black hair swirling around his head.

"We should have left an hour ago," said Taukie, glaring at his partner as he gripped the handlebars of his machine with his sealskin mitts. "We'll never make it home by tomorrow in this weather."

Mikkigak didn't care. He had no one waiting for him back in the village, but he understood his partner's anger. The delay would cause Taukie to miss his infant son's birthday and worry his wife.

"We can still make it back in time if we drive fast," said Mikkigak. "The blizzard should hold off 'till we get to the shack."

Situated an hour's ride away, a small shack and its propane stove would keep them warm until the weather passed.

Taukie nodded with a begrudging expression before pulling up the hood of his bright blue parka. Both hunters knew the truth — out on the frozen ocean, a *piqsiq* waits for no man.

Visibility approached zero, distance and direction lost in the diminishing contrast between white and grey. Taukie fired up his engine first, turning the vehicle and its heavy sleigh around in a wide arc. Their snowmobile tracks had been buried beneath the freshly drifted snow. Mikkigak mimicked the actions of his partner. Without a cumbersome sled attached, he took the lead and the two men drove off in the direction they thought they had come from.

After riding blind for nearly an hour, a flat patch of darkness materialized from the whiteness in front of Mikkigak's snowmobile. He jammed his brakes, barely able to avoid flying headlong over his handlebars into the open water. Impossible, he thought. The *sinaaq* was kilometres away. Had they somehow turned back towards the floe edge in the bad weather? Flailing his arm, Mikkigak waved Taukie to a stop before throwing his own machine into reverse and cutting the handlebars to the right.

Once turned around, he pulled up alongside of Taukie, their machines facing in opposite directions.

He yelled over the raging storm: "We're heading back where we came from."

Mikkigak pointed into the blustering snow where the open water had been visible moments before. The gale carried his voice out across the tundra, away from Taukie's ears. He moved closer until the fur trims of their hoods nearly touched.

Before Mikkigak could speak, the ice shook beneath their snowmobiles. A grinding roar diminished the rumble of their engines. Beneath them, the firmament shifted, settled again, and then tilted in the other direction. Panic flashed across Taukie's face. Mikkigak steadied himself on his machine, bracing for the worst. Huge slabs of ice fractured and split around them, cracking into shards with resounding explosions. The ice pan they were on tipped with the weight of the snowmobiles, suddenly free from the main floe that held it steady on the water's surface.

Mikkigak gunned the throttle. His machine hurtled towards the widening gap between the smaller pan and the main ice floe, skipped across the narrow ribbon of dark water, and landed on the safe side. Looking back, Mikkigak saw that Taukie had leapt from his machine and struggled with his trailer hitch. Taukie kicked in vain at the thick build-up of ice on the pin that secured it. The extra weight of the caribou and sled prevented him from skimming over the open water. A squall of snow obscured Mikkigak's view, only to have Taukie materialize a second later, frantically waving both arms and rushing towards the near edge of the drifting pan.

Mikkigak's scalp tingled beneath the hood of his parka, his body surging with adrenaline. He had an opportunity, albeit fleeting, to speed across on his snowmobile and grab Taukie before the pan floated away. Mikkigak whipped his machine around and gunned it back towards his partner. He stopped at the edge of the floe and stared down into the frigid dark water, the black ribbon widening with every passing second. Both men had skipped further distances across water before, even as children growing up together. If Mikkigak kept the throttle open, his machine would easily carry him across without sinking. He could grab Taukie, turn the snowmobile around on the wide pan and they could skip back across together before the gap became too broad.

"*Ikajuq!*" Taukie shouted, the wind suppressing his voice. *Help!*

Mikkigak looked up at Taukie, then back at the gap between the pans. In the time between glances, it had grown to the length of his snowmobile. Mikkigak had a single moment left to act. He revved his engine and the wind died for a heartbeat as if the storm had paused, waiting to see what Mikkigak would do. Taukie rushed towards him on the retreating pan. Mikkigak's pulse throbbed in his ears, his breath coming fast and shallow. The toxic fumes of the idling engine filled his lungs. *Now or never*, he thought.

But he hesitated.

A cold plunge into the freezing ocean meant certain death. He couldn't swim. His boots and his parka would drag him down into the bottomless depths. Mikkigak peered down into the dark water between the men. Fear brought trembling to his arms, loosening his grip on the throttle. Taukie and Mikkigak locked eyes. His trapped partner's expression changed from desperation to one of incredulity.

As the pan drifted beyond reach, Taukie shouted in Inuktitut. "*Suma?*"

One word, over and over: *Why?*

The wind swept back in. A swirl of blowing snow engulfed Taukie and the drifting pan. Then came the groan and the fracture, followed by a horrible and dreaded crackling, so loud it rumbled in Mikkigak's chest. He watched in horror as the pan broke into pieces and Taukie tumbled into the freezing water. Through the thick blowing snow, he could not see his partner any longer, but he heard Taukie scream once before being drowned out by the grinding of the ice.

When he felt a tremor beneath his machine, Mikkigak turned and fled.

Spring is known as a time of suicide in the remote north. While the darkness of the frigid winter would seem the likely candidate for driving a troubled mind to end its suffering, it is more often the return of the Arctic summer and its endless sunshine that brings out thoughts of unease, discontent, and despair.

Mikkigak stood beneath a clear April sky on the frozen ocean. It had been a full year since the death of his hunting partner. As he sipped tea from the lid of his thermos, the hot liquid warmed his bones, staving off the chill that came from a day's ride across the bay. Killing himself was the farthest thing from his mind.

Less than ten steps behind him, his companions burst out laughing, shouting in Inuktitut about an earlier mishap caused by the youngest of the hunting party. Their search for polar bears had been unsuccessful, but the good weather and the familiar company had kept everyone's spirits high. Mikkigak ignored their laughter and settled himself on his parked snowmobile. He withdrew his heavy rifle from the sling and laid it on the seat behind him. Bathing his face in the midday sunshine, he surveyed the landscape.

Snow-covered mountains rose from the eastern horizon and endless flat ice stretched across the western frontier. The lack of contrast between the low-hanging clouds and the sparkling snowscape obscured the horizon. He rubbed his fur mitten against his sunburned cheeks.

In the days after Taukie's death, he had roamed the land, lost in the blizzard. A rescue team found him twelve miles north of the village, delirious and exhausted, needing to be flown south on an emergency medical plane for frostbite and dehydration. He had constantly protected his hands ever since. Badly frostbitten skin was more susceptible to the cold.

Now, while he sat staring at the landscape, Mikkigak discerned a dark shape against the white backdrop of the nearby hills, standing on a raised area of land. A caribou, he considered, before dismissing it as being too small. A cairn of stones, perhaps? No, there were no *inuksuit* in this area. He leaned back and pulled his binoculars from the secure box on the back of the snowmobile. Removing the protective caps, he focused them across the bay towards the hillside, but the object had vanished. Mikkigak lowered the lenses and scanned again with the naked eye. The shadowy form came back into view, having been perhaps hidden for a moment by a squall of snow on the distant slope. He raised the binoculars again, keeping a keen bearing on the location as he did so. A lone figure, parka hood up, stood motionless on the white landscape. Mikkigak blinked rapidly to relieve his eyes of the strain of the sun's rays, losing sight of the stranger in the process. The man's machine must have broken down. It would take months for him to walk back to the village from this distance.

Before he could turn to the others with his discovery, a firm hand clamped on Mikkigak's shoulder, startling him. The youngest of the hunters, Abraham, picked up the thermos from which Mikkigak drank and sniffed it before setting it back down. His face was grim with deep creases in his dark, weather-worn skin. A thick halo of wolverine fur encircled his face, wicking moisture away from his nose and mouth.

"Caribou?" asked Abraham, joining Mikkigak in staring at the hillside.

Mikkigak scrunched up his face, a common way for the Inuit to indicate the negative without speaking. Flustered, he tried to resume his scrutiny of the figure he'd seen on the distant hillside, pointing in the direction for the others to see.

"There's a man up there," he said, handing the binoculars to Abraham. The younger man held the lenses up for a long time, adjusting the focus and scanning back and forth.

"There's no one up there," said Abraham.

Mikkigak tried again with both binoculars and naked eye, but he couldn't find the man. "He was up there. I saw him."

"Just like those rocks yesterday, that you thought were walrus." Abraham patted Mikkigak's shoulder and walked to his own snowmobile. The group laughed at their comrade's expense, while they packed up their belongings. Mikkigak laughed along with them, nervously. Perhaps he was tired. Or maybe the sun on the hillside had fooled him somehow.

Before Abraham fired up his snowmobile, he snickered and said: "We're headed in the same direction as your man on the hill. So we may cross paths with him."

Shame rippled through Mikkigak. His old partner would never have made the same mistake about the rocks. Taukie had been a true hunter and Mikkigak knew he had hunted in his partner's shadow.

As the snowmobiles of the hunting party departed across the frozen ocean, Mikkigak's mind drifted back to when Taukie slipped beneath the cold, dark water and the same terrible emotions stirred within him. The engine's rumble vibrated in his chest. His forearms ached from the shuddering of the handlebars.

On the long ride home, he wondered what exactly he had seen on the hillside. That lingering fear and the shame of his cowardice threatened to overwhelm him. He thought about the thickness of the ice over which they rode. It had to be fifteen feet thick at least. And yet, somewhere deep within the deafening roar of the machine, he swore he could hear a chasmic grinding. In response, he gunned the throttle to catch the others, and as he did so, a high-pitched whine rose up from the hum of his engine that sounded eerily like a scream.

Mikkigak rounded the corner into the baking aisle. Instrumental music crackled from the overhead speakers. He hummed along absently. Leaning on his half-filled trolley, head down, he examined his grocery list.

"Good morning," said Ooloota in Inuktitut. His head snapped up at the sound of her voice. Taukie's wife lingered in the centre of the aisle with one child standing in her shopping cart, while another peeked out shyly from behind the hem of her parka. Her tired smile did little to distract from her wan complexion and bleary-eyed expression.

Mikkigak stammered, unable to respond.

"I haven't seen you in a while," she said. "How are you doing?"

Warm blood rushed into his face. As she spoke, he found himself transfixed by the three-year-old boy in the cart. The toddler's features resembled Mikkigak's late friend. He fixated on the boy's eyes, seeing only Taukie's within them. Reaching out instinctively, he grasped the infant's tiny hand and took it in his own. The boy tore his fingers from Mikkigak's grasp and, in so doing, fell backward in the shopping cart. The child wailed, thrashing amongst the groceries. Ooloota rushed to his aid and cast a worried glance at Mikkigak.

He pulled a wad of cash from his jacket pocket and held it out for her—an offering she didn't understand. Ooloota stood, clutching her howling child while her daughter clung awkwardly to her legs. Both children wailed and she looked at her husband's friend with bewilderment as he dropped the cash onto the aisle floor and fled towards the checkout.

Mikkigak rushed out of the store and through a cluster of loitering teenagers. Frozen breath and cigarette smoke hung above their heads in a thick cloud. Descending the stairs quickly, he swung his arm to scatter the ravens foraging at the bottom of the steps.

A group of ravens is called an 'unkindness'. Mikkigak felt the name suited them. They always tore up his trash before the garbage truck arrived, or woke him before dawn with their gurgling croaks and shrill calls, clattering across the metal roof of his house.

Flustering the birds had made him feel better, but that heavy feeling of shame lingered. Taukie had been a great hunter, relentless in his pursuit of every animal he encountered—bear, wolf, caribou. Without someone to provide for his family, Taukie's wife and children now relied on charity and meagre government cheques to shop for food at the local supermarket. Shame at the sight of her had driven Mikkigak out the door, leaving his unpurchased items in an abandoned shopping cart.

Beneath a clear blue sky, a light breeze carried the cold air. Mikkigak felt refreshed as he shuffled down the icy road towards his house. A familiar voice called out to him. His uncle Piita.

"Haven't seen you for awhile," said Piita. "You been outta town?"

"Not since I was medevac'd on the plane last year," said Mikkigak, turning away from the store, eager to hide himself in case Ooloota and her children came outside.

"Ah, after the storm. You're very lucky to be alive. I still think about Taukie. He used to bring me fresh food after every hunt."

Mikkigak raised his eyebrows high and held them there for a few seconds, an Inuit version of a Southern nod. He forced a smile and the two men stood in silent reflection, staring at the snow as it drifted down around them.

If the people of the town had placed bets on their survival, they would have wagered on Mikkigak's body at the bottom of the ocean. Taukie had been a survivor. At two years old, his mother had gotten drunk and left him outside in the snow while she slept on the living room floor. Wrapped only in a towel, he lay there for hours until a cousin, dropping by to visit, had found him. Taukie had spent months in the hospital, recovering. In later years, his adult skin bore the damage that the harsh climate inflicted

Mikkigak slumped his shoulders, glanced down at his hands. The lesions of his own frostbite had faded away to nothing. The word *coward* surfaced in his mind. He swallowed hard, his throat thick with mucus. Mikkigak had told everyone that the storm had separated him and Taukie. Right now, he longed to tell Piita what had really happened.

"The ice fog is rolling in," Piita said, pointing out towards the frozen sea. "You think the plane will be late today?"

Mikkigak didn't answer. He stared out towards the sled dogs, chained into the sea ice with heavy metal spikes. The dogs lay still atop their houses, up off the cold snow, curled into tight balls of protection from the wind. A figure in a hooded blue parka stood among them.

Mikkigak blinked rapidly, stuttering as he pointed towards the man on the ice.

"What's wrong?" asked Pitta, laying a hand on Mikkigak's shoulder.

He jerked back at the older man's touch, pointing again to the lone figure. "He's coming for me," said Mikkigak, his eyes wide and frantic.

Piita followed the line of his nephew's finger out towards the dogs, squinting into the coming fog. "Who is coming?"

Mikkigak didn't try to answer.

He dashed away towards the safety of his home.

A vicious Arctic gale ripped through the tiny hamlet that night, snakes of blowing snow slithering down ice-covered roads. The cold had dipped to minus thirty-five. Windchill at that temperature would leave exposed skin with frostbite in mere minutes. All of the buildings at this latitude were constructed on metal stilts driven deep into the permafrost; the frozen soil would not allow for concrete foundations. Even the largest of them shifted and swayed in the wind.

Mikkigak's home was no different, shuddering and creaking with every violent gust. Inside, a lone bulb glowed beneath the range hood on the stove and the electric heaters kept the chill at bay. Mikkigak snapped the deadbolt closed on the front door and leaned against the frame for support, his legs unsteady and knees aching. An aroma of canned mushroom soup hung in the air, mingling with the stale odors of cigarette smoke and perspiration. His gut churned, unsatisfied. Shambling across the linoleum floor, he slumped into a kitchen chair and pressed his sweaty palms to his tired eyes, holding them there until bright lights sparkled in the darkness behind his lids.

As he shook a cigarette out of the pack and lit it, his mind drifted back to the figure out on the sea ice. Perhaps it was Abraham, or one of the others, playing tricks on him. Or perhaps his guilty conscience reshaped his vision, warping it into a tangible form. Pushing himself to his feet, he splashed warm water on his face at the cluttered kitchen sink.

Through the frosted kitchen window, Mikkigak had an unobstructed view of the deserted street, which stretched out into the darkness. Not a soul afoot. He pulled a clean towel from the oven door handle and used it to dry his face before looking again. Across the street, white smoke billowed upward into the night sky from his neighbors' chimneys, the full moon glinting off the steel rooftops. Lights glowed dimly behind curtains in every window. Beyond the houses, a blanket of darkness obscured the sea ice.

Before turning back to the room, he hesitated. Something was off, out of place. Someone stood in the rift between the houses, backlit by the low moon. The shadow of the figure, impossibly long and thin, stretched out towards his house, the peak of its hood barely touching the bottom step at Mikkigak's front door. His breath stopped at the sight of it and all feeling in his legs drained out from under him.

Taukie.

The lit cigarette slipped from his trembling hand and he fumbled to catch it, burning his palm as he crushed it in his fist. Mikkigak swore profusely before rummaging through a cluttered drawer, selecting the largest knife he could find, unsure of what good it would do. When he rushed back to the window, the figure had vanished.

Mikkigak scrambled from window to window around the house, bumping into walls and furniture alike, scanning outside frantically for any sign of his dead partner. He tried to open the back door in hopes of escape, but the drifted snow held it firm. The back windows were frozen shut and too high to jump without breaking a leg. Panic set in. He leaned his forehead against the cold glass of his bedroom window and chuckled in a shaky desperate whisper. He felt weak, his mouth dry.

There had to be a way to make peace with his former hunting partner. There had to be a way to spare his own life. His mind whirled with possibilities before settling back on the failed encounter with Ooloota in the store. He scrambled across the room to the telephone. He would call her, confess his failure to save Taukie, confess his cowardice and pledge his life to help her and the children. Taukie couldn't seek revenge if he knew his family would have no one to help them. With trembling fingers he punched in the familiar digits and pressed the receiver to his ear. One ring. The spiral cord only extended halfway across the kitchen, preventing him from seeing out into the street. Two rings. He frantically determined what he would say to her and how he would say it. Three rings. *I let him die. I could have saved him, but I didn't.* Four rings. *I'm a coward and a liar. I'll take his place, I'll provide for you all. Anything it takes to make him stop.*

The phone clicked loudly as if someone picked up, but there was only silence. Mikkigak held his breath, waiting to hear Ooloota's voice, but there was only the sound of the grinding ice, deep and rumbling through the crackling of the telephone line. He screamed in terror, high and effete, before yanking on

Relentless

the phone cord, pulling the wall unit free from the plaster. It smashed to the floor, breaking to pieces as Mikkigak collapsed to his knees with his head in his hands. A high-pitched, frenzied wail escaped his lips, while he scanned the room for a possible escape.

The drone of a distant snowmobile brought him standing to attention. The medevac plane, he thought, his mind whirling before shouting the idea into existence. He could flee to the South, thousands of kilometres away where Taukie could never find him. He dashed to the front door, grabbing his coat from its hook and stepping into his winter boots. When he touched the cold surface of the doorknob, his fingers curled back.

He couldn't leave. Taukie was right outside.

In the darkness of the living room, Mikkigak moved to the window to check the alley across the street for any signs of his former friend. Out there, on the icy street, below the house, Taukie stood waiting with his hood pulled down low and his arms limp at his sides—ten steps closer.

Mikkigak screamed into the glass, his breath fogging the surface of the window. A flood of incoherent phrases and obscenities spilled from his mouth as he stomped around the kitchen. He threw his head back and wailed at the ceiling tiles. He couldn't walk to the airport, or even the health centre. He couldn't even leave the house to jump on his snowmobile. The knife trembled in his tight grip. He needed something to steady his nerves. Something to clear his head so he could think of a plan.

He groped under the crawlspace through a hole in the closet floor. He found the neck of the container he had hidden there. A bottle of home-brewed liquor, half-full. Mikkigak cradled the plastic bottle in his hands, staring at the clear liquid inside as the strategy materialized in his mind. He set the homebrew down on the kitchen table and snatched a large tumbler from the cupboard. Pouring himself a stiff drink, four fingers highs, he pounded back the liquor in two quick gulps. The vapour burned his nostrils. Heat flooded his face.

Inside the front door, beneath a pile of old rags, stood a canister of lamp oil. He heaved it up and onto the table, placing it down next to the booze. He slugged back a second glass of

100

equal measure. It burned a little less this time, numbing his nerves even more.

He grabbed the cordless telephone from the charger and dialed the crisis line. After five rings, a woman's voice responded.

"Hello, what's your emergency?"

Mikkigak steeled himself with a deep breath, trying hard not to look at the oil canister on the table in front of him.

"I've burned myself. Really badly. I'm going to need a medevac." His voice slurred as the words came out, and he was surprised at how quickly the alcohol had taken effect. "And an ambulance."

There was a long pause, then keyboard clatter on her end of the line before she spoke again. She recited his address and asked him to confirm it. "I've notified the authorities and help is on its way," she said. "What part of your body has been burned?"

He hung up the phone without answering and rushed to the window.

Taukie stood at the base of the stairs outside of the house, his face concealed by the fur-trimmed hood. Mikkigak screamed in terror, hauled in a deep breath and screamed again. He threw the phone towards the wall where it shattered in a dozen pieces.

The emergency crews would be there any minute and he needed to be injured in order to be medevac'd. There was no time to waste.

One arm, he thought. *Just my arm. That will be enough.*

He downed a huge gulp from the homebrew bottle and slammed it back down on the table. His hands shook. He pulled on a jacket to lessen the damage from the burning fuel. He splashed the lamp oil across the arm of the jacket. Was it enough? He had to make sure he would be flown out. He splashed a bit more, cursing as it soaked into the leg of his pants and spattered on the floor. He grabbed the lighter from his pocket, holding it aloft with his thumb at the ready.

He struck the flint.

The blaze surged high and bright, singeing his eyebrows and lighting up the entire room. The pain was not immediate, but when it came, it arrived with such force that Mikkigak screeched and howled and threw himself sideways into the kitchen table, toppling it over and sending its contents crashing to the linoleum floor. The liquor and lamp oil splashed and emptied. He fell in a heap, his flailing arm catching the fluids. His lungs burned with smoke. Fire engulfed the kitchen. Unable to breath, Mikkigak rolled and swatted at his burning clothes. Blinded by the pain, he staggered to his feet and threw himself towards the front door. He tumbled down the front steps, crashing into the snow at the bottom.

From there it was all a blur—the sirens, coloured lights flashing against the white snow, the voices of the emergency crew—until he lost consciousness.

Most of the patients on the recovery ward were asleep. Hot air blasted into Mikkigak's hospital room, fluttering the curtains like startled ravens. He rolled gingerly onto his unburned side, staring out the darkened window of his private hospital room. The red taillights of a passing plane blinked their way across the clear night sky. Two weeks had passed, but he felt no better than the night he'd arrived. Pain had been absent while he slept, but settled back in as the analgesic fog wore off. Tingling pinpricks danced up his legs. Mikkigak, growing restless, rolled onto his back and remembered the relief he felt when the evening nurse administered his injection hours before.

"Hello?" he cried out to the passing shadows in the hallway beyond the opaque window in the door. "Anyone there?"

Mikkigak strained to reach the dangling call button with an extended arm. The delicate, tender skin beneath his bandages stretched to the point of tearing and he gritted his teeth against the sting. One finger, then two, slipped around the device, and he was able to pull it close enough to grasp it fully. His head lolled back on the pillow after the struggle. With a long exhale, he clicked the call button downward.

As he released it, movement caught his eye. At a second glance, the corner of the room lay empty, filled only with shadows. A flicker of light from the window perhaps, or the fading anesthetic playing tricks with his mind. Yet, despite his doubts, an unmistakable presence persisted, lingering in the heat of the room. He lifted his head as far as he could and stared into the darkness. He pushed the call button again, unsatisfied by the subtle clicking sound it made.

His head slumped onto the pillow again, his neck muscles tired. Down between his feet, toes pointed at the ceiling, a figure emerged from the darkness. Mikkigak's pulse quickened. The pain that had resided in his legs swept up into his torso, causing spasms as it travelled. He pressed the call button a third and fourth time.

The figure took a single step into the light of the window frame, its features hidden in shadow. Mikkigak shut his eyes tight and pressed the button again and again. New scents, familiar odours—gasoline, the musty pelt of caribou and its fetid meat—overwhelmed the hospital room.

Mikkigak's heart raced, his blood pumping through his veins. Heat flushed into his face, his chest constricted. He squeezed his eyelids shut, until he heard the cracking of the ice.

His eyes snapped open. Taukie approached the bed, his hood lowered, his skin waxy and yellow, tight across bones and skull. Like dried animal hide. Mikkigak saw no rage in those features, no lust for vengeance. Only a lifeless, dull face with dead eyes fixed on Mikkigak.

Taukie's parka, dark and wet, dripped streams of water onto the tiles beneath him. Taukie opened his mouth to speak and a low rumble rose up from within him, a grinding of ice. Dark liquid poured from his gaping jaw, spattering on the floor.

Mikkigak let the call button fall from his fingers and he screamed. The sting of the burns amplified. His body on fire all over again. A nurse burst into the room, switched on the light. The monitor next to Mikkigak beeped faster and faster. The nurse rushed to his side, barely avoiding Taukie's outstretched hands. The sound of the grinding ice grew louder and louder. Strangers gathered around his bed—doctors, nurses. Unfamiliar faces all around him in the bright light of the room. Everyone shouting at him, hands clutching him, pushing him down onto the bed. He couldn't see Taukie anymore. He flailed, pain ripping through him.

Relentless

The sound of ice buckling and shifting filled the room. Pain exploded in his chest. The high-pitched, continuous tone on the machine replaced the frantic beeping.

Mikkigak shut his eyes, feeling cold hands pulling him down through the mattress, deep into the icy, dark water.

Sins Of The Father

By Colleen Anderson

H e was like Rasputin when they took him down. Sixteen bullets rammed into him while he peeled the flesh back from his last victim, loyal to his art until the end. Nine women in all he murdered. That last, too, did not survive. How could I correlate this reality with the loving father I had known?

He was more than just loving. He paid attention, read me stories, played chess and Frisbee toss with me. We went for walks, discovering flowers, trees, the unique patterns of clouds. Little did I know that he was using those outings to search out more intriguing specimens. He was quiet, attentive and a good listener. That too, I learned later, was how he teased out the pattern of his victims, like a detective dusting for fingerprints.

My mother was no harpy who drove him to seek revenge on women. They displayed tenderness for each other that was as delicate as a butterfly's dance through blossoms. They went on weekly dinner dates to moderately tasteful restaurants, leaving me in the care of a babysitter. To many people, including my mother and me, our life was perfect.

Sins Of The Father

Father victimized far more than nine women, of course. Those nine were the ones he tortured, and who did not have to live with the knowledge of what had been done to them. But he also seared the memories of those hapless women's families and friends. The horror was like the gap where a rotting tooth once sat, always being probed. No one ever thinks of the murderer's family, the unnoticed victims. My mother and I bore our scars and wounds, and our shame. The awareness of what he had been resided within us, germinating, giving us nightmares as we eternally replayed the possible reasons, what he had really felt for us. It was another way for him to inflict his dark desires, a legacy we could not purge. My mother withered away, her world chopped down like a forest's last tree by a heartless logger.

I grew up and changed my name. At St. Paul's Hospital, at the West End's edge, I cared for the ill. I changed bedpans, administered medicine and held the hands of the dying. Through the glossy linoleum corridors, the hushed hum of the rooms, I tried to gain strength and resilience in my psyche, understand the aches of the world, and lessen the painful throb that accompanied my heart every day.

St. Paul's borders the areas of disease and destitution. Those who prowl the streets or have found a home amongst refuse because their minds aren't fit for our institutions; those who swim in the fluids of their downfall; they are always around us, coming into the ER, courting death. Meanness and pettiness, greed and fear walked and limped through those doors. But sometimes they had a worse disease, just as my father did. Evil grows.

It was one of those dreary days when Vancouver weeps at the degradation of those in the Downtown Eastside, whose livers are eaten by the worm alcohol, or their minds by the needle-borne demon. I made my usual rounds to each patient's room, doling out their medications. I saw a hunched figure, definitely not her daughter, enter Mrs. Wylie's room. I went to check and there, a man, grizzled and rank as the alleys, was pulling a ring off her finger. She flailed weakly, her withered hand grasping at him. He smacked her and pushed her hand away.

As she cried out, I yelled, "Hey! What do you think you're doing?"

The man turned, his hair like greasy snakes, and smiled. Then he thrust me aside and ran into the hall.

For a moment, I forgot about my duty to the patient. Anger did not burn me, but something more fearsome—hate. A numbing cold raced through me. Like the dark fungus that reaches out in dank and mouldering apartments, it took hold and blackness haloed my vision. I smashed the door open into the stairwell. Leaping down two steps at a time, I gained on him.

Shadows curled as I grabbed his collar. It barely registered that my fingers were charcoal-tinged. Twisting my hand into the fabric, I slammed the scumbag into the wall. The tamped down hate and fear rushed through me and out my fingertips as they brushed his neck.

For a moment, all went black as a heavy blankness and confusion filled me. Then with absolute clarity, I saw every crime and dirty thought this creature had ever committed. Kaleidoscopic images flashed—taunts, beating dogs, sexual abuse, injecting viscous fluids, punching out a store clerk, losing jobs, more fights, jail, alcohol, fiery drugs. A panoply of pain and fear flooded me. My distilled fears flowed back to him. Locked, we were a conduit neither could break. We danced and jittered in the flickering neon stairwell, puppets together. After a minute, an eternity, it ended. The destructive mould that had surfaced in me had now transferred to him. He crumpled to the floor, tears searing runnels through his dirt-smeared face, snot a slug's trail over his chin. He cringed and cowered, still shaking.

Rooted, I stared at a black fungus that had dried and powdered from my fingertips. I wasn't marked, but he was. Spots tinged his neck and hands and he whimpered as he scrubbed at them. Moments passed before I could snatch the ring and retreat upstairs, leaving him to an unknown fate.

I fled the hospital, complaining of a sudden illness, and locked myself in my apartment. I looked out my window onto English Bay, staring at the innocent white sails of boats, the joggers running along the waterfront. While I looked on the placid beauty I tried to tease out the tangled web of my thoughts.

I'm not a religious person. What has god to do with any of it? Why pray to a deity that gave his creatures free will and vowed to not intervene? And if he could intervene, then he was a sick bastard who let monsters like my father etch nightmares into people. It was what my father had called himself, when they found his meticulously written diaries. The Etcher, for he wanted to carve each canvas of human skin with his words, his teachings. He never did explain why he did it, what drove him. It was all about technique and recording lessons. Is madness the same as evil? He was both, but what sort of monster was I becoming?

My father's blight had long since infected my soul, and it had welled up at last, leaving me neither mighty nor euphoric. I had been choked with nausea, but had been relieved when the hate had erupted from me, transforming into a wicked fungus like that which poisons dwellings in the soggy environs of the coastal rainforest.

In nature, mould is green, filled with chlorophyll, or brown and part of the rotting and renewal of vegetation. A natural cycle devoid of desire and deviation. But black mould feeds on the urban falsity of lies and plaster, the sins of betrayal and duplicity. It grows in the moist corners of gyprock, unseen behind couches and TVs. It permeates lungs and airways too, slowly eating at the dwellers until their mysterious illness is identified.

I was a product of my heritage and the land. Vancouver had claimed me, and somehow, I had been chosen to exact revenge for the deeds of my father, and perhaps others. I wondered if my father was responsible for more victims who had gone missing and were never found. There were so many more than nine dead souls claimed by the man I knew.

I am my father's child. What happens to us in childhood shapes us for the future; the genetics, the environment, the love or abuses that touch us. I was made of love and horror. My father had betrayed us, a monster, a wolf in sheep's clothing, and I would never be able reconcile the split that had made up his whole. It's why, once I uncovered my power, I did what I did.

I took to prowling Vancouver's destitute areas, on side streets where prostitutes decorate the sidewalks like forlorn flowers, around Main and Hastings where decay and wasted lives spill out like industrial sewage, in alleys moist with human refuse where the crystal meth addicts try to consume others before they are consumed. I took shifts as one of the street nurses who aid those in the Downtown Eastside. An itch grew in me, a feeling beneath my skin that I could alleviate only through movement. I did not consciously seek out evil, but there is always evil in such places. Perhaps we are drawn to it unconsciously, as a plant seeks the sun.

Something drew me. As the weeks passed, it became more persistent. I had to peer behind that dumpster, look in that stair-well. Sometimes I found a person in need. Sometimes I found more.

One night, while my co-worker tended to a passed-out man in Chinatown, I felt compelled to explore the alley behind the red- and gold-lettered shops. I almost stumbled over the man raping a scrawny, unconscious woman, his hand clamped over her mouth. He didn't even stop when he saw me.

The cold swept down on me black and frigid. It singed my veins and cleared my sight. Without thinking I hauled him off the woman, throwing him into the brick wall across the lane. He slid down as I stood over him. I wanted to squeeze the horror from him, but stopped with my hand on his throat. I would not be my father.

Instead, I pressed my fingers into his cheeks, increasing the pressure as his eyes came into focus. He scowled and reached up to my hands, but by then the black lanugo was creeping up his face. This time, time slowed and I watched the progression. He clawed at my hands, but I held on. We locked together as the change took place. His face furred like some wolfman's, and his sins played out their reel to me, each bloody interaction; preying on drug addicts, weakened people. A parade of raped women. He had not cared if they had lived or died. I did not care if he did.

He went slack, his hands falling, drool slipping down his chin, eyes wide, staring. I screamed at the barrage of images, oblivious of the presence of any observers.

This time, only he juddered as I exerted more pressure, the black fungus crawling down his neck, under his shirt. A call halt-ed me. My co-worker. Breathing deeply, trying to bring light in-to my mind, I released my grip and turned away. The victim hadn't moved. I knelt, feeling for her pulse, pulling back her eyelids. Dead.

After the police dealt with the situation, I returned home. Sitting on my bed, fingers wrapping over my eyes and anchored in my hair, I rocked back and forth. What was I? What was I doing?

It felt as if someone had threaded sutures under my epidermis and gently tugged on them. While not painful, the need to move constantly crept through me. I could not sit still. The blackness in my fingertips faded away unless I hated. So I used it, filtered it, and turned my hate into a lesson for others.

I became a reluctant vault for all the terrible deeds of those I touched. No longer just my father's exploits, ow I festered with a cinema of misdeeds. Night sweats soaked me, my stomach roiled. The more I tracked down the aberrant and infected them with the mould, the more I had to do it, to unleash the images that infested me.

I began to patrol the tracks by the sugar refinery, away from downtown. The large grey concrete cylinders look more like Cold War silos than a place to harness sweetness. Metal walkways, high fences, hidden cameras and the hulking shapes of railway cars added a disturbing, destitute mood. On the other side, away from the walkways, the inlet's oily waves lapped parasitically at the concrete as if it were a salt lick. The water sloshed and made throaty sounds.

I could not say why I was drawn to such an area, forlorn at the best of times, except for that strange intuition now hauling me here and there. The area whispered of neglect and sinister secrets. Mesh fences, razor wire, barred doors, and the sharp thorns of blackberry tried to hedge out the graffiti, the burned-out tins and piles of refuse that indicated a garden for the abandoned. Shadows were thick here, even in the day. At night, they were impenetrable. I carried a flashlight, but left it off, walking softly, listening, feeling.

A train tunnel led from the south, to the bridge over the water. As I drew near, noting a security camera's shiny black eye, I smelled the salty fecundity of the ocean. The throaty sound now seemed more like a slurping, and my footsteps slowed. Dread quivered my belly, for the water was hundreds of yards away, and the sound in front of me, echoing against the night-painted sides of the train tunnel. Shadows bulged, bloating and rippling. I wanted badly to shine my light, and just as much not to know what was there.

No longer able to wait and listen to the sad whimper of infinite pain, I flicked on the flashlight, its white beam wavering. Legs, a shadow, warty lumps, a green sliminess, black—no, red—puddles; a slideshow of images revealed in the unsteady light.

Did Newton say, to every action there is an equal and opposite reaction? My father's heinous actions led to my reaction, the ability to inflict the memory of one's deeds back upon them. But just as I had this power, could my deeds too, create an equal and opposite force? Somehow, I felt certain that this reaction hunched in front of me, salty seaweed wafting from it, making me swallow, and breathe through my nose.

The thing hissed and gurgled, turning. It was half woman, naked, beautiful, terrifying, dripping dank water from silvery hair. But the light highlighted a face that shifted, eyes that shone like a maddened horse's, a nostril flaring, nightmarish teeth and a thick tongue lolling and dripping bloody gore.

What lay beneath the creature twitched, his face half-eaten, an eye lying bare like an oyster in the shell of bone. I retched, bile hanging stringy from my lips. Half crouching, I advanced on the monster, forcing the black mould to my fingertips, but I hesitated. Did I really want to see the horrors in this thing's mind?

I had a mission; my father had branded me with a mark of shame and I could not shy away because of squeamishness. The thing trudged toward me, its victim dragged behind like a broken pull-toy. The man wasn't conscious, but his hand adhered fast to its scaly greenish leg. I grabbed for the creature's throat and a jarring cold jolted my veins. Its scaly skin felt moist and tacky, but the fungus tried to turn away, back up my hands. It was hard to see. My fingers slid off the slime.

The rotting seaweed stench permeated me as I tried to grip the monstrosity's neck again. Before I knew it, I was heaving up everything in my stomach, over and over. The creature ignored me, flowing over the ground, toward the water under the bridge, its meal in tow.

It took me hours to return home, stopping to gag up a bitter residue. Shakily, I turned the key and staggered inside, sliding down the door. I managed to get to bed after rinsing my mouth.

The next two days I was pale as a water-bloated corpse and couldn't keep anything down. I had met my nemesis, a monster so terrible that it turned me to quivering jelly. I had not helped that poor wretch and considering his state, it had probably been better he died. I shuddered and slipped into uneasy sleep. Eventually, the shakes and queasiness subsided and my thoughts bobbed to the surface.

Was I really responsible for bringing another monster into the world? I would have stopped then and there, but the irresistible prickle within tugged me to restlessness. The fresh air and the rain made me feel better. I took to walking often under the perpetually leaking sky that can hit Vancouver for weeks. I identified with my city in a way I hadn't before, learning the layout of the streets, fascinated by the architecture and age of neighbourhoods. Shaughnessy's rich and sometimes empty old dames, Chinatown's quaint yet slightly dilapidated buildings mixed with the new, East Vancouver's bohemian chic, the nondescript blandness of Champlain Heights.

I learned crimes happen anywhere. Not every alley or derelict building holds wickedness. The city, like any forest, houses those that prey and are preyed upon. There were always lawbreakers, but a jaywalker or a speeder did not deserve my fungal touch. In fact, there had to be a true touch of evil for the mould to take hold and dance the greater sins through their minds and mine. Fungus needs darkness in which to take root, so then why had that creature by the tracks managed to resist my touch?

I came across those whose vices were made evil by the drugs that took them over. Crystal meth morphed people into savages, and the drug nicknamed "bath salts," though as of yet infrequent, was worse. I hoped that the parade of past exploitations would move them away from a destructive road. Addicts were rarely evil, just desperate, but when I came across true malevolence it felt like rusty spikes being driven through my viscera.

Months passed and many monsters were jailed with my

help, usually scratching and gibbering as the black fungus took root. The lesser evils, I left where I found them. I did not really judge them. The mould did that. And I was not free of the acts perpetuated. I knew exactly what they had done and that nest of vipers weighed me. My mistake was never wondering what happened to that lanugo that spotted their flesh.

One afternoon, as the rain fell steadily and cold, I walked the seawall around Stanley Park, the pewter plate of the ocean flat, obscuring its denizens. The sky melted into it, the drizzle creating a marriage of greys. October was fully entrenched and the season had descended like the apocalypse. Leaves mouldered to treacherous sludge on the roads and walks. Worms writhed, drowning in their besoddened homes; mildews acted like it was a night at the ball. Only the hardy, like the jogger who passed me, braved the dreary climate. He nodded to me from beneath his jacket's hood, and ran on, a companion against the weather.

It was the fact that it was still day, though dreary, that lulled me. Deep in thought, I nearly stumbled over the creature pulling itself over the railing by the lighthouse, its grey and green scaly hide sluicing water. I backed away, watching it. Silver strands of hair hung like rivulets of cascading water. It turned flat brown fish eyes upon me, the horselike countenance baring massive, sharp teeth, large nostrils flaring. Then it shifted, like wind skimming the surface of the ocean, so subtly that I almost doubted my eyes. The snout flattened, the eyes grew bright, the figure straightened. A lithe woman, with skin the colour of chrysoprase, hair silvery and tangled, ambled toward me.

No matter what the illusion, the fetid miasma of seaweed, rotting fish and dank cellars hit me with the truth. My mouth watered, bile surging and I swallowed, breathing through my mouth. I'd seen this same creature that night by the tracks. Had it been coming up to snare an unwary jogger or was it hunting me?

I backed up farther. The crawling surge of mould moved through me, tingling my fingertips. I wasn't sure I'd have any affect. I was about to turn and run when another jogger came up behind me and passed with head bent down. I yelled, but she didn't see the monster.

Lightning-fast, it snapped out an arm and the jogger went down. She lay stunned upon the path, rain pelting her face. The creature bent toward her. My stomach pitched, but I had no choice. I clasped its shoulders, forcing the mould upon its body. Again, the fungus wouldn't stick and my hands slipped off, but it hissed and turned toward me, swatting out at the annoyance disturbing its meal. I ducked and came around from the other side, panting as I tried to keep from vomiting.

It knelt by the woman and her eyes finally focused, going wide. She pushed at its chest and her hands adhered where mine had slid off. Its wicked teeth approached her face and she screamed.

I kicked its head and tried to choke it from behind. It elbowed me and I fell, vomiting, onto the concrete. I crawled back and laid my hand on its back, hating, loathing, calling up all the anger within, the horrendous deeds of past fiends, and channelled all the blackness through my fingers. They grew warm as I pressed my palm on its back. No images came to me.

Something sizzled and the thing screeched, arching back. It whipped around and a large webbed hand pushed me. I flew back, my head smacking soundly into the railing. Struggling, I could not swim through the darkness that pulled me down as the jogger shrieked.

When I came to, pain and horror surged out of me. I rolled to my knees and dry-heaved into the pouring rain. I looked around, but only a thin scarlet streak trailed over the walkway, past the railing and to the rocks below. The rain was washing all evidence away and the sea thing had returned to its lair. There was no point calling 911, when I had neither victim nor perpetrator.

Sick, shivering, I made it home and suffered the same symptoms as before.

My father had a good life—his naive, loving family and freedom to pursue his morbid delights. I tried to lead a good life, do what was right, atone for his sins, but I'd lost all my friends, and I'd isolated myself with my feverish searches. *Feverish* was what I felt, for I itched and sweated, always trying to dig up the wickedness that skims just beneath the city's veneer. Is a person who generates mould slowly consumed unless the fungus can be spread? I had done precious little to stop that thing from the water.

As inevitable as the sun setting, we would meet again—and we did. This time it came hunting me, not some hapless pedestrian. I walked home along Burrard Street and under the bridge along the waterfront, past the aquatic center and the high-rises. Vistas of the ocean and the breezes seemed to cleanse me, clear my sinuses that clogged now if I stayed indoors too long. The green grass cushioned me as I strolled and for a while I could forget the ebb and flow of sinister influences. I just was, a part of the natural world, an organism moving through.

Early morning and the sun dried the tears of dew upon the grass, a rare nice day for the time of year. A chill added clarity to the air, and a few hardy sailboats and the freighters farther out waited to move on their journeys.

I felt the monster before it touched me, for my stomach twisted and tossed as if the calm seas had sent their storms internally. I whipped around, striking with an outstretched arm and a closed fist. The beast lost its balance as my fist struck its head. I wasn't foolish enough to think I had bested it. It tumbled to the ground, catching itself on a long clawed hand, and kicked out. I jumped back, and spit out some bile that surged up my throat. Breathing through my nose, I called on my ability to manifest hate into the fungal pitch that bloomed at my fingertips. It wasn't enough.

I poured revulsion and fear and anger into my hands, tugging on that invisible thread that wound through me. It felt like having stitches removed, an unpleasant beneath-the-surface movement of alien material. Gritting my teeth, I concentrated as the fish thing advanced on me. Its dead milky eyes stared straight ahead and a long eel like tongue moved over fleshy horse lips and sharp-edged teeth.

My fingers darkened and the lanugo moved up past my wrists. I had hurt it once before. I ran at it pushing my hands into its chest, knocking it down as I straddled its rotting hide. Screaming, I poured my horror into it. It shrieked like a thousand bats being torn apart and black wisps wafted from its chest. The odour of kelp and seaweed and dead shellfish filled me and as my gorge rose, it batted me off. I fell and twisted to my side to vomit. Then the monster latched its teeth through my coat and into my arm.

I howled as scarlet oozed out onto the blue fabric. I used my boots to try and kick it loose, and clawed at it. Wounded, its strength lessened and I managed to back away, crawling across the ground.

Something slammed through my brain and laced my nerves with acid. I couldn't even scream, as I convulsed. I wouldn't have known if I had been devoured at that moment.

The fish-horse thing was shaking its head, stringy hair spraying water everywhere. I tried to focus, gasping for breath. Something had happened. Gathering my wits, I staggered to my feet, wondering where all the early morning joggers were. Alone with this watery demon, I tried to summon the mould into my hands, but nothing happened. My arm dripped thick blood and the monster righted itself, growling now in pain or anger. It didn't matter; its goal had not changed.

Backing away, disgust and fear filled me, but the summoning would not come. Something bumped into me and I cringed. I sidestepped so that I didn't put my back to the greater threat, and a shape—possibly a man—stumbled forward. From his head sprouted a two-foot long stem, brown and black, wrinkled, fuzzy. Gluey fluids leaked down his head, seeping into his grimy collar. Flaps of his scalp hung down, where the growth had sprouted through.

He moved between me and the monster, and reached for it, his hands adhering. The creature snarled and slashed at him, and then there was another shambling man. I recognized this one, also with a protruding stem from his head. He was the first one, who had tried to steal the woman's ring. Lanky, taller than the first, he too shuffled forward.

Gaping, I saw the stems were mushrooms, fungal growths. They were my fruiting bodies.

The second man grabbed the fish thing and adhered to it as well. It bit his arm and fluids, yellowish and clear oozed out. A third juddered in. Not one looked at me or each other. Mindlessly, they grabbed the monster, their eyes dull. It could not remove them. They pulled it down on the grass, all rolling around. A fourth joined them and I realised they had all been criminals I'd stopped, the ones who had not been taken by the police. I could only wonder if the ones sitting in cells now banged into bars, blindly seeking escape guided by the growth sprouting from their brains.

Numbed, I watched as the thing hissed and snapped. Skin tore loose, greyish and pink, but they didn't stop. They managed to pin its limbs, and while three held it the fourth opened his mouth and stuck his tongue between the pried-open horse jaws. He coughed into the fish-thing's mouth and it squealed.

The revolting menagerie dragged the convulsing monster over the grass and onto the sand. They didn't stop but moved into the silvery water's mire until nothing remained.

Shuddering, I went home and did not leave my apartment for four days.

The tugging left me, as did the power to bring on mould. Spring came and flowers bloomed. Was my ability seasonal and would it return with the fall rains? Was I no better than my father? I thought I would stop those criminals, and I had, but turning them into zombies had not been my intention. I do not know if I'll be able to use the mould again, but I'm afraid to. My father decided he could take lives. I did the same. I fear to use this power, if it returns. Perhaps then, I will be the sacrifice to assuage the sins of my father, and the black mould will consume me from within.

Snow Angel

By Nancy Kilpatrick

They'd been warned in Whitehorse. By several people. And again in Dawson City. But Joe never listened. He called himself a "free-floating spirit." Coleen thought of him as somebody who needed to be nailed down to the earth.

Joe's death had come as a complete shock. Coleen was just finishing drying and putting away dinner dishes in the Winnebago's little cupboards. He stepped out of the one-man shower that also functioned as the toilet. She pushed aside the pink and white curtain above the sink to watch the odd snowflake drift onto the frozen tundra, thinking again how much she did not share his love of or trust in this barren land. It had been his idea to come way up here in the Fall, "when there's no tourists," he'd said, adding in his poetic way, "so we can nourish the snow spirits and they can nourish us."

She folded the dishtowel. "We're almost out of food, Joey. We'd better head back to Dawson City—that'll take us half a day. Didn't that guy on the CB say something about a low pressure system building?"

When he didn't answer, Coleen turned. Joe sat on one of the benches at the table, a deck of cards before him. His chunky six-foot frame slumped back towards the front of the vehicle. His pale green eyes looked as cold as the crevices in a glacier. In his right hand he held two mismatched socks.

Coleen performed mouth-to-mouth resuscitation. It didn't work. She got out the first aid kit and found some smelling salts. When everything else failed, she pounded hard on his chest, first in desperation, then in hysteria.

All that had happened yesterday. Today she had a different problem—what to do with her husband's rotting corpse.

She stared out the window. The storm she feared had magically eaten its way across the landscape while she'd struggled last night to revive Joe. She had judged the weather too bad to drive in, but now she realised she'd made a mistake by not trying. Eight hours had done damage. Swirling gusts of snow clouded her view beyond a couple of yards. Every so often, the wind banshee-howled as it buffeted the two-ton camper, threatening to hurl everything far above the permafrost and into another dimension. It made her think of Dorothy being swept away by the tornado and ending up disoriented in Oz.

Coleen's eyes automatically went to Joe's body. She had wrapped him in the two sheets they'd brought along and se-cured the sheets with rope. He lay on the floor like a tacky Hal-loween ghost, or a silly husband playing ghost. Any moment she expected him to rise with a 'Boo!' Then he'd laugh and admit to another of his practical jokes. But the form refused to play its part. It did not sit up. She had an urge to kick it in the side.

"It's all your fault!" Furious tears streaked down her face. She snatched at the box of Kleenex and blew her nose long and loudly. "*You* wanted to go into debt to buy this stupid camper. *You* wanted to drive all the way to the Arctic Circle. *You* wanted to stop at this dumb lake. You never plan anything. Why do you have to be so damn spontaneous?" She yanked open the small door beneath the sink and hurled the tissue into a paper bag of burnable trash.

Suddenly, her shoulders caved in and she let loose. The weeping turned to a wailing that frightened her all the more because it made her aware that she was alone. She stopped abruptly and the silence hurt her eardrums. When had the snow and wind expired? Outside it looked like some kind of perverse fairyland, white on white merging with a colourless sky. Although the Winnebago was warm, she shivered. This place. It was so… empty. Nothing could live here.

Coleen knew she needed to act to break this mood. She washed her face in the kitchen sink, dried it with her shirttail and tried the radio again

Last night the storm had smothered signals coming and probably going too. For the first time since Joe's death, she was getting static. She reread the part in the manual about broadcasting. She picked up the microphone and sent out a distress call and gave their location, as recorded by her in the log—three hundred kilometres north east of Dawson City, on Hungry Lake. She repeated the call for over an hour until she needed a break. Coleen sat at the table with her coffee. She felt disheartened and lifted the cup to inhale the comforting sweet-roasted scent. Sweet-sour noxiousness clotted her nostrils and she gagged. "Oh my God." Setting the cup down spilled its contents. Joe was starting to stink.

Primal fear raked a nerve. She jumped up and lifted the seat of the bench. Among the tools inside she found a small shovel and the ice axe she'd insisted on buying. She threw on her parka, stepped into her boots and grabbed the fur-lined mitts.

Once she was dressed, she turned the knob of the back door. The door wouldn't budge. The glass had frosted so she couldn't see the problem. Panicked, Coleen threw her weight against the door, finally creating an inch gap that let in freezing air. She peered through the slender opening. Snowdrifts had climbed half way up the camper. She jammed the shovel handle between the door and the frame and used it as a lever to pry another inch, then another; finally it was wide enough to get the axe through. Hacking and ploughing gave her a one-foot opening she could lean around.

Crystalline whiteness extended as far as she could see. The banks must have been four feet high, the lowest drifts two feet deep. The realization dawned that the truck would not get through this. Even if she managed to connect the chains to the snow tires—and there was a good chance she couldn't do it by herself—no way would the camper make it.

Despite warm clothing, the air nipped at the skin on her face until it numbed. A bad sign, she knew. She pulled the door shut and made herself another cup of coffee.

While Coleen drank it, she thought about her situation. The weather might warm. The snow could melt enough in a week or so that she could drive. She'd keep working the radio; eventually somebody would hear her.

The thought came, *maybe a snowmobile will drive by, or a dogsled*, but she knew that was the way Joe would think. There were only 25,000 people in the whole of the Yukon, and Hungry Lake was a good hundred kilometres from the nearest highway.

Thank God she'd bought that book on surviving in the Yukon when they'd passed through Dawson City. Joe, of course, had laughed at her. There was a checklist at the front— *What to do While Waiting for Help to Arrive*. She'd torn it out and tacked it to the wall. Joe had found such practicality even more amusing.

Joe. She knew she'd been avoiding thinking about him. She sighed, but it sounded more like a moan. Her heart felt both too full and empty. She looked at the body on the floor, wrapped like a mummy. Even now the smell was there, under everything, seeping into the air like poison spreading through water. She'd have to take him outside.

After trying the radio again, Coleen dressed in the heavy clothes—this time wearing a ski mask as well. She continued chopping and digging into the crusty snow. By five o'clock she had the door wide open and the bar locked so it would stay that way. The landscape looked the same now as it had at ten a.m., as it would look at ten p.m. With only six hours of darkness, even the underside of the clouds reflected white luminosity— snowblink, they called it. This almost endless brightness was unnatural. She remembered near-death stories she'd read about, of white light and how departed souls float down the tunnel towards that blinding light. Coleen wondered if Joe had gone down a tunnel. She squinted. She couldn't imagine anything brighter than this.

Dense cold filled the Winnebago, which numbed her nose and anesthetized her emotions, making the second part of the job easier.

She grabbed Joe's ankles. Despite the gloves, she was aware of the hardness of his cadaver. Coleen clamped her teeth together; this was no time to let grief and fear overwhelm her. Grunting, heaving, she dragged his dead weight along the brick-red linoleum to the back door.

There were snowshoes—she'd seen to that—and she strapped a pair onto her boots. She'd never walked in them and had no idea how she'd manage. They weren't like skis; they were feather light, but the racket part up front was so wide that she couldn't help tripping.

Her big fear was that the snow wouldn't be solid enough to hold her up, but it did. She backed out of the camper and, once sure she was balanced, bent over and grabbed Joe's feet again. She pulled and the rigid body slid over the doorframe easily. All but the head. It caught on the frame. When she yanked, it plummeted into the trench she'd created around the door.

Joe was so stiff that when his head went down into that pit, it jarred her hold and the rest of his body popped straight up into the air.

Look, Collie, a human Popsicle!

Fear slid up her spine. Coleen looked around. Nothing. No one. Only the corpse.

She knew he was dead, but still she said, "Joey?" and waited. It had to have been the wind. She steeled herself and jumped up to grab his feet. Her body weight pulled them down. He levelled like a board and, stepping backwards carefully, she slid him along the compacted snow.

Somehow she didn't want to leave him just outside the door. The dry cold was exhausting, and deceptive—she knew it was colder than it felt and she had to be careful of frostbite—but she dragged him away from the camper, tripping once, having a hell of a time getting back up on the snowshoes. The air burned its way down her throat and the pain in her lungs became ferocious, making her fear pneumonia.

Finally, he was far enough away that she wouldn't smell him every time she opened the door, yet he'd still be within sight.

Coleen struggled back. By the time she got inside, her en tire body was numb. That desensitization was preferable to the defrosting that followed. A hot shower brought pins and needles pain that made her cry out loud. Trembling, she bundled up in Joe's two bulky sweaters, pulled open the bed and crawled in. She couldn't see Joe from here. She drifted into what turned out to be a nightmare. A frozen animal carcass with Joe's face grinned down at her. He was sucking on a decaying Popsicle.

When Coleen woke it was still light outside. She checked the battery-operated clock radio and could hardly believe she'd slept nearly twenty-four hours, until she moved and her muscles screamed and she remembered having been up for thirty-six hours doing exhausting work in sub-zero temperatures.

Joe's death, her being stranded, all of it suffocated her with despair.

It was only the thought, *I could die here!* that got her out of bed.

She ate, played with the radio—now even the static was gone—reread the survival list, and went about doing what was necessary. She checked all propane hook-ups and turned the heater down—she'd have to use the gas sparingly. Thanks to Joe, the extra tank had been gobbled up when he'd insisted they extend their stay.

Next, she tried the engine. It wouldn't kick over; the fuel line had to be de-iced first. She'd need to do that twice a day to keep the battery charged. The gas gauge needle pointed to three quarters full and there was a five-gallon container for emergencies. Two of the three hundred kilometres back to Dawson City would be through the mountains where the snow could avalanche and put out the road. But at least there was a road. Making it to Highway No. 5 was the problem. They'd had a hell of a time getting through the spruce and poplars to the lake from there and, under these conditions, there'd be double hell to pay to get out. And all of it depended on enough of a thaw to drive the camper.

The snow, she realised with a bitter laugh, had at least one benefit—there would be plenty of snow-broth; fresh water wouldn't be a problem. She checked flashlight batteries, matches, candles, flares and medical supplies. The cupboard held a big

Snow Angel

jar of instant coffee and a box of tea bags, but even at half rations, the food would only last one person one day. They should have been back in Dawson City five days ago, but Joe had insisted on this side trip. She'd argued against it, but he'd fixed on some crazy idea he'd read about in a magazine that he could fish in the lake and catch char and they'd "negotiate with the Eskimo gods to live off the land," a concept that now struck her as insane.

During most of their fifteen-year marriage she had, in her way, loved Joe, although their relationship was not the fulfilling one she'd hoped for. She had to admit that because of him she'd been places and done things she wouldn't have, left to her own devices. Early on, she'd seen him as a welcome contrast: devilish to her seriousness, adventurous to her timidity. But it wasn't long before she admitted that what had once been charming traits in Joe turned to juvenile habits that gnawed away at her patience; divorce had crossed her mind.

Still, he was her husband, 'till death did them part. He had died, if not in her arms at least in her presence, and he had died as he'd lived—impulsively. On some level she missed him dearly.

But she was also angry. Angry that he'd brought her to this God-forsaken place and left her, maybe to slowly starve, or freeze to death like a character in a Jack London story. And why? Because he claimed his destiny was to see the "Good and Great White North." He had too much childish faith that life would support him to worry about freak storms. If he wasn't already dead, she might have entertained murderous thoughts.

She pressed her face against the chilled glass in the back door. White. Everywhere. So pure, so foreboding. The wind had erased her tracks. She couldn't see Joe's body. Suddenly, she felt guilty for leaving him out there all alone in an icy grave. The thought struck: *Maybe he's not dead. Maybe he's in a coma or something.* She tried to talk herself out of that notion, but soon Coleen was putting on the parka and the snowshoes and trudging across the hardened snow in the direction she thought she'd taken her husband.

The air held a peculiar and enticing quality. The cold felt almost warm. As she crunched along, the beauty of the

124

snowscape struck her. Everything was elementally pure, pristine. Blameless. Almost spiritual. In the darkening sky, a faint aurora borealis flickered green and blue, like some kind of signals emanating from heaven. She understood how Joe's soul could soar here. Suddenly, the incredible glare on the horizon temporarily snowblinded her.

From behind, the wind resurrected itself and knocked Coleen off her feet. She plunged straight forward, as if her body were jointless. Her face crashed into the frost and knocked out her breath. As she struggled to her knees, little puppy yaps came out of her mouth. Pain shot through her nose and forehead. She squeezed her eyes shut hard and opened them slowly to regain her vision. The snow beneath her was red. She touched the ski mask over her nose; the glove was stained.

Coleen looked around wildly, trying to orient herself. Joe's body lay six feet away. She started to think, *Why didn't I notice it before...* and then stopped. The body looked the same, but the snow surrounding it appeared scraped. It reminded her of being a child and lying flat, making snow angels by opening and closing her legs, and raising and lowering her arms above her head. *He can't be alive!* she thought. *The sheets are still tied around his body. There's no way he could move his arms and legs.*

Coleen crawled to the body. Instinctively, she felt afraid to touch it, but forced herself. It was iceberg hard. When she tried to shake him, she discovered that the sheets had adhered to the snow crust.

"Joe! Joey!"

Freezing in Spirit Land, honey.

"My God!" She tore at the sheets, but her gloves were too bulky so she yanked them off. Still, the cotton was more like ice and she had to use a key to gouge through it. She wedged her fingers between the fabric and his neck and ripped the fabric up over his chin. The cotton peeled away from the familiar face to reveal chunks of torn flesh and exposed frozen muscle.

Coleen gasped, horrified. His face was a pallid death mask. "Joe!" Her hands had numbed and were turning blue, and she stuffed them back into the gloves before slapping his cheeks. "Can you hear me?"

She sobbed and gulped stabbing air. The storm was getting

bad again; she could hardly see the Winnebago through the frozen fog of ice crystals. If she didn't go back now, she might be stranded here. She glanced down at Joe. If he hadn't been dead when she'd brought him out, he certainly had suffered hypothermia and died of exposure. The wind whispered and Coleen accepted the fact that Joe had not spoken to her.

She left him and clumped her way back. By the time she shut the door and peered through the glass, the camper was enshrouded in white air.

Coleen devoured the rest of a tin of sardines in mustard with the last two saltines and drank another cup of coffee. The coffee had her edgy and she decided to switch to tea, although she didn't like it as well. Now that the solid food was gone, she'd need to keep her head.

All day she'd tried the radio and reread the *Survival in the Yukon Guide*. She'd just finished an improbable chapter on snaring rabbits by locating their breath holes in the snow and was about to close the book when the section on leaving food outdoors caught her eye. The three paragraphs warned about wolves, bears, caribou and other wild animals being attracted to food. She laid the book in her lap for a moment and rubbed her sore eyes. Human bodies were food. She recalled seeing the movie *Alive* and how the survivors turned to cannibalism. She shivered and hugged herself. Coleen went to the door. Snow, the voracious deity of this land, lay quiet and pallid, waiting. Somewhere out there was her husband's body. Those marks in the snow crust could have been made by something that was hungry. Something that might at this moment be gnawing on Joe's remains.

She shuddered. He deserved better than that. Maybe she should bring him back indoors. But that thought was so bizarre it led to the toilet and her vomiting up sardines.

By the time Coleen felt steady enough to put on the heavy outdoor clothing, she knew what she had to do. She gathered the supplies she'd need and went to Joe.

The snowscape had turned into an icescape—the Winnebago was icebound. That should have scared her, but she felt strangely invincible and coherent, her mind as crystal clear as the air. There were no tracks; she found him by instinct.

She opened the cap on the lighter fluid and doused his body. It was hard to believe that under this frozen earth lay huge oil deposits; the nauseatingly sweet combustible reeked. She struck a match and dropped it onto the pyre. Flames sprang upward and black smoke fouled the air. She hoped the snow gods did not feel defiled.

Coleen stared at the fire charring her husband's remains. Flesh crackled and a familiar scent wafted up; she realised that she had never known anyone who'd been cremated. It came to her that maybe his spirit was trapped in his frozen flesh. If any body possessed a spirit, it would have been Joey's.

As the inky cloud danced heavenward, she panicked. Maybe she was doing the wrong thing. Maybe the flames would not just cook his flesh but would burn his soul. Maybe hell was... Something caught her eye.

A pale spectre appeared in the dark smoke. The face was luminous, the form familiar. She watched Joe ascend like a snow angel. He smiled down at her and waved. Coleen sobbed and waved back. Tears welled over her eyelids and froze on her lower lashes and she stepped closer to the fire's warmth. *We all do what we have to, Collie.* He'd said that often enough, but this was the first time she understood it.

She felt bone chilled. The wind confided in her—the northern demons were still hungry.

Coleen shovelled snow onto the flames and they sizzled into silence. As darkness crawled up the sky, she worked quickly with the ice axe. There was plenty of meat. It would take time to pack it in ice and store it safely before the storm returned.

The Delivery Boy

By Judith Baron

id-January, night-time. Minus twenty-seven with an extreme cold alert. Peter McCain, a young man from Gravenhurst, Ontario, wished he didn't have to work the late shift at the pizzeria. Weather like this could get a guy killed... or at least drive him crazy.

He preferred summer months, working at the golf resort by Muskoka Beach, which overlooked South Bay's small cluster of islands. The season's colours inspired him to paint, too. He favoured painting to dropping off pizzas or picking up golf balls, but until he made a name for himself as an artist, menial jobs would have to do.

At nine p.m., a big order came through by phone. The address landed right on their delivery zone's border cut-off, so technically they could decline; but five extra-large pizzas and two-dozen fried wings equalled good money on a slow night, so his boss, Henry Ravello, insisted. The customer had opted to pay when the food arrived, and Peter hoped he would get a good tip. Bringing someone pizzas and wings in this weather? He deserved it.

By a quarter past nine, Peter drove off in the company car with a big red insulated bag on the passenger seat. According to Google Maps, the travel time totalled fifteen minutes, which gave him a half-hour window for any traffic or human error within the forty-five minute delivery guarantee.

He pulled up to the lot, the coarse and loose gravel crunching under his tires. His eyes surveyed the charred house in the middle of nowhere. His jaw dropped. He double-checked the address. He didn't want to call Henry and sound like an idiot, especially since Henry took the order himself. He used the GPS in the car and Google Maps on his phone. Both confirmed he had the right location. When he tried to look at the house on Google Earth, however, the satellite picture showed an empty lot. How could that be?

Engine off and headlights on, he mounted the steps to the front door, carrying the pizza bag. He winced as the wooden steps creaked under his weight. His nose wrinkled at the smoky smell. The headlights from his car bounced off the door's surface, producing a reflective glare, beckoning him to open it. On the brick wall next to the door, the number and street sign matched the address he had: 121 Mulberry Road.

He rang the doorbell. It left a sooty mark on his finger. He waited a minute, and knocked on the shiny door.

"Hello? Pizza delivery!" Peter yelled.

He repeated himself four times. By then, the forty-five minute guarantee had nearly expired. Could this be a prank? The online prepayments of today had almost phased out these antics; with cash on delivery orders, though, some restaurants still experienced this once in a blue moon.

He needed photographic proof in case Henry gave him grief. He took out his phone.

Suddenly, it went dark all around. His headlights had gone out. No streetlamps. Clouds hid the moon. He had to turn on his phone's flashlight.

A shadow scurried from the car to the house.

Laughter. Children's voices, all around. Panic filled him. Peter shivered, the cold numbing his face. He tried to call Henry, but his phone had no reception.

Stay calm.

The Delivery Boy

At that moment, the front door creaked open.

He pushed the door open halfway. Darkness, except for a faint glow towards the back of the house. He used the light from his phone to look inside. While the exterior appeared scorched and reeked of smoke, the interior of the house, with its ornate furniture, looked like a page out of a Pottery Barn catalogue. And it smelled of gingerbread.

Nobody answered, but he could hear the laughter of young children behind him.

The door opened all the way.

Curiosity took over him, and without even thinking, it commanded his feet and carried him forwards into the unknown.

The door slammed shut behind him as soon as he entered, its draft swaying his pizza bag.

Footfalls.

A group of small people gathered before him, the biggest one no taller than five feet. They smelled like freshly harvested potatoes.

Peter aimed his cell's flashlight on one of them, and gasped—it looked like a mandrake, with vaguely human facial features and a root-like body dressed in children's clothes. He moved to look at another one in a red dress holding up its hands—only the hands looked like stumps, with no fingers.

He shone his phone around him and saw more of the same.

"What the—" Peter mumbled. His eyes must be playing tricks on him.

A tall shadow moved about at the back of the house and swayed in the flickering glow. All of a sudden, the lights came on, catching him off guard. Even the mandrakes let out a shrill, piercing the silence. They scampered like cockroaches in the presence of light, retreating to the staircase.

He screamed, and the mandrakes stared at him with their lipless mouths agape.

"Oh, you cry babies!" an adult female voice boomed from

the kitchen.

He heard the sound of the oven being opened and closed in quick succession. The strong gingerbread smell tickled his nostrils.

A tall woman in a soiled apron traipsed towards Peter. She had a thin frame, her olive skin slightly lined and her nose curved like an eagle's beak.

"I see that you have just met the children." She spoke with a slight accent, something that sounded Latin-based.

Children? Peter looked at the mandrakes again, and even though he never wanted to admit to this, he nearly peed in his pants.

"I'm Peter from the pizzeria and I've got your order right… here," he stammered and pointed at the red bag in his hand.

"Nice to meet you, Peter. You can call me Maribel. What trouble, for a night like this! Come on in, why don't you? I have just baked some gingerbread cookies and we can sit down for a chat over a cup of tea, no?"

The *children* looked at Maribel, and then at Peter, waiting for his reaction. Maribel nodded at the children. Within seconds, the children swarmed him. The smell of soil and roots overpowered him and he wanted to gag. He started to doubt his own sanity. He hadn't smoked a spliff in a week, so he wasn't high; and even when he got high, he never imagined walking mandrakes.

"Look, I got your order here, you can pay me now so I can get back to work and then go home," Peter said.

"But I insist, Peter. I just baked the cookies. Why don't you try one? My daughter used to love them. Plus, may I point out that your headlights are out?"

Peter shuddered. Did she have something to do with that? He had other questions, but the children started to push him towards the kitchen with Maribel leading the way, as if she knew he had no choice but to do what she asked. He began to panic as these children muttered words he couldn't understand. It sounded like Spanish or Italian. They corralled him deeper into this nightmare.

"Ma'am, I really must go now!" Peter protested.

The children's hands—he used the word *hands* loosely; they

had no clearly defined fingers—started digging into him a bit more. Thankfully, he had his full winter gear on, but he could still feel the pressure of their collective grip.

A basket of gingerbread cookies and a tea set awaited him at the kitchen table. The cookies smelled pungent with cinnamon and ginger. Maribel sat down and gestured him to sit as well.

Maribel pointed at his hat and gloves. "You don't need to keep those on."

As much as he had no intention of staying, he did as she asked. Maribel had a way with her talk—somehow, he could not defy what she asked. He put the red bag on the table but no one seemed to care about the food he brought. Had she been expecting him all along? Just then, he saw one mandrake standing behind her. This one looked different from the others—its features appeared more defined and human, with green eyes and a few tufts of brown hair where the leaves should have been. The hands had extra stumps that looked like fingers.

"Peter, meet Alex, and Alex, Peter brought us our pizzas and wings!" Maribel turned to address the mandrake with a name.

He felt light-headed. It must have been the gingerbread or cinnamon smell. Normally, (not that one would normally walk into a house full of talking mandrakes) he would have run away screaming; but to his surprise he said hi to Alex the mandrake.

Alex came out from behind Maribel and smiled—a strange sight as the lipless mouth curled up and the eyes became slits—and thankfully, no handshakes.

"You see, Peter, Alex is my *grown* daughter," Maribel said.

He looked at Alex and gasped. He rubbed his eyes and stared again. The image didn't change.

"Peter, why don't you sit and have some cookies and tea with me? We can chat about plants, if you wish. You see, I am a botanist. I know how to grow just about anything, including the ginger in the gingerbread cookies."

He sat down. It became clear to him why she called Alex her *grown* daughter. She obviously grew all these mandrakes, but didn't address the elephant in the room: like how could these mandrakes walk and talk like people? And why did she keep insisting that he eat her gingerbread cookies? What did she put in them?

The other mandrakes hovered behind him at the threshold of the kitchen, blocking his only exit. He looked around and saw a large, framed picture of Maribel, a man, and a little girl on the wall. The little girl wore a purple dress, and had the same aquiline nose just like Maribel. She must have been under twelve. Judging from the hairstyles and clothes, the photo could have been taken before Peter's time, in the 1980s. Alex bore an uncanny resemblance to the girl in the picture.

At this point, Peter gave up hope for a tip. He needed to get out now!

"Look, I'm just going to call for a tow truck. I won't say anything to anybody. Keep the pizzas. Enjoy the food and drinks on me. *Please.* I'd like to leave now," Peter said in a shaky voice that even he didn't recognize.

"Okay, go ahead, Peter."

Peter tried to use his phone, but it did not turn on. He pressed the home button frantically, then the power button, to no avail. He wanted to swear, but how could he in the presence of these children? That would be—

Rude?

No, it would be crazy.

This whole situation, his entire train of thought, *crazy.*

When he stopped trying to turn his phone on in vain, Maribel looked at him the way a cat eyed a bird.

"You should have eaten my cookies," she said. "Now we will have to do it the hard way."

Suddenly, a brown stump stuffed his mouth. Alex's "hand." It tasted bitter and earthy. He felt lightheaded and saw colours swirl around him. His heart thundered. The rest of the mandrakes swarmed him from behind and carried him on his back out of the kitchen, past the hallway and down the stairs into the basement. He tried to spit out Alex's hand, but she shoved it into his mouth harder, choking him.

Then he could see no more.

The Delivery Boy

Lying on his back, Peter awoke in a basement that felt warmly humid. Tied to a wooden table, ropes tightened around his hands and feet. Winter jacket and snow pants gone. The chemicals coursing through his veins caused everything in his field of vision to blur, elongate, distend; the room transformed into a demonic funhouse: the span of exposed joists ran at uneven angles, the pink insulation between them dripping like taffy; the transom window, a rectangle of breathing glass that inhaled into a bubble, then exhaled back to its normal form.

He had vomited while unconscious. The taste coated his lips. Some of it dripped down the side of his chin.

Squinting, his eyes helped a little to alleviate the hallucinations. He looked around. The walls hadn't been sheeted with plasterboard yet; there were only squares of insulation stuffed between two-by-four studs. Heat fans and heat lamps surrounded him.

About ten feet away, there was another table, also surrounded by fans and heat lamps. A human body in a soiled purple dress lay there. Some sort of brown root, covered in leaves, had grown out of a cavity in the stomach. The body's hands, mossy and covered in dirt, hung limply over the sides of the table.

No. It couldn't be. This had to be an illusion caused by the chemicals.

He squinted rapidly, again and again, hoping to dissolve the horrific sight. The corpse, with a tree growing out of it, didn't go away or change to something he could explain.

I'm really seeing this.

Peter wanted to scream, but he feared that Maribel and her mandrake children would return. He needed to escape. But how? As he tried to wiggle his hands and feet out of the ropes, he looked around for something within grabbing distance that he could use to free himself. A knife maybe. No such luck.

Footfalls.

Creaking down the stairs.

"*PLEASE!* DON'T DO THIS!" Peter shouted. "My boss knows where I am. He'll send someone to find me. Just let me go. *PLEASE!*"

Maribel appeared at the bottom of the stairs.

She held a scalpel.

"Peter," Maribel said soothingly, "this will be over quickly and it does not have to be painful."

He had no recourse other than to beg.

"What do you plan to do to me? Please. My parents. They'll be devastated!" He tried to appeal to her as a parent, and then grimaced at the thought of her being the mother to all these mandrakes.

Maribel ran one hand over his stomach in a non-sexual way, like a butcher trying to figure out how to make a good cut in the meat.

Despite the heat lamps and fans, he felt cold and cringed.

It dawned on him that Maribel had every intention to use his body to grow mandrake children.

"Look, Maribel, you already have Alex, why do you want to grow more? Please, just let me go, I won't say a word to anyone. I swear."

Maribel studied Peter silently for a few seconds, as if considering his proposal. Then she spoke. "I have only girls, Peter. Alex wants a boy. I need a boy to grow boys."

Maribel held the scalpel to Peter's body. She lifted his thermal shirt to expose his stomach. He began to cry.

"Please don't! DON'T! I BEG YOU! PLEASE!"

He jerked his body as violently as he could, trying helplessly to free himself from the ropes.

"Stop moving! Or I'll really have to use this!" Maribel yelled while holding up the scalpel.

The mandrake minions swarmed the basement, filing in from the stairs and standing by close to Peter. One had a long straw, and another had a burlap sack in what passed for her hands. She gave the sack to Maribel, who put it over Peter's head.

"NO! STOP! DON'T" those were the last words he remembered speaking before someone hit his head, knocking him out.

Andrew Gamble tucked his pen back in his notebook after Peter McCain finished his story. This poor young man had been out in the extreme cold for who-knew-how-long, and had obviously lost his mind.

The Delivery Boy

"I swear, officer, I swear all I have told you is true!" Peter McCain pleaded. His normally rosy complexion looked ashen now, his lips white and chapped.

"Kid, just get some rest for now," Gamble said, giving Peter a fatherly pat on the shoulder. "People who have gone through hypothermia can experience strange things. The condition of the body can affect the mind, you know?"

Gamble exited the room and strolled to the nurse station in the central part of the intensive care unit. He went up to a nurse and asked her about Peter. She found Peter's admission report and gave it to Gamble.

As he looked over the report, the nurse told him a summary of what they'd found.

"He had hypothermia for an undetermined length of time, but no blunt-force trauma to the head. Surprisingly, though, he had no frostbite in such an extreme weather condition. We did find a substance that corresponds to his claims of having ingested trace amounts of mandrake, which is a hallucinogen. With the combination of hypothermia and hallucinogen, it's not unusual for someone to believe something this strange has happened."

Gamble nodded as he flipped to the last page of the report. "Thank you," he said to the nurse without looking at her. "I assume someone will take him home?"

"His parents will take him once he's discharged. He woke up screaming several times and said he had mandrakes growing out of his stomach. We have ordered a psych evaluation and we can't discharge him until the evaluation is complete."

"Thanks," Gamble said as half the nurses rushed off to respond to a code blue.

He exited the hospital. The sun was radiant, a welcomed sight in the midst of a savage Canadian winter. He got into his vehicle and went over his notes.

What if the kid had hallucinated the mandrakes and the house, but *not* Maribel, his attacker? People with compromised mental clarity often imagined seeing things, but the attack itself could still be real. On the other hand, Peter McCain sustained no blunt-force trauma to validate his claim that someone had knocked him out. He didn't even have any cuts, which negated the idea that someone wanted to slice him open and grow mandrakes in his stomach.

Besides a prank pizza order, an extremely cold night, and Peter ingesting hallucinogens, the story lacked credibility.

But what about the lack of frostbites? Sure, Peter wore his winter gear, but at minus twenty-seven plus wind-chill, even a seasonably dressed person would still get frostbite after exposure for an indefinite period of time. If Peter had arrived at nine -thirty, then he would have been exposed for nearly two hours in the cold as someone found him at eleven-thirty that same night. Perhaps Peter told the truth, that someone kept him inside a house much of the time?

Also, Henry Ravello, the owner of the pizzeria, had personally taken the order and mentioned the customer's accent. Perhaps that bit of info had been shared with Peter in advance, later serving to inform his hallucination. Gamble tried to call the phone number used to place the order, but the number did not work. That could have been explained by a disposable cell phone, which pranksters often employed.

So many questions went through his mind. He had to wait for Grant Williams, his partner, to get back to him about the supposed house the kid entered, and any Maribel living in the area with a daughter named Alex. For due diligence, they needed to dig up records—if any—pertaining to the address where Peter ended up. There could still be an attacker at large.

He drove back to the station and started typing his report on his computer. His cheeks turned red when he typed out what Peter McCain told him, nearly verbatim. He told himself he had to report exactly what the victim said, however ridiculous it sounded. So far, the case had not been classified as anything other than a person being found unconscious in the cold. No theft had occurred; his colleagues found the entire food order in the pizza delivery vehicle. After reading what he'd just typed, Gamble did not think he had anything to investigate, other than a young adult ingesting a nonindigenous hallucinogen.

His phone rang. Williams.

"Gamble, I'll be damned. Fire in 1983. No fatalities—no one lived there at the time and it burned to the ground," Williams said. "This kid could have known about it though. It made the headline news back in the day, and his folks could've told him.

"When I went to the city hall to look up the land registry, I couldn't find anyone named Maribel. Nothing had been built there ever since. That hag Bertha McLaren hovered over me the whole time—she said a child died in that house and the grieving parents split up and moved out before the fire. You can always count on that busybody for these things, even something that happened thirty-five years ago. Gamble? Are you still there?"

Gamble remained silent for a few seconds after Williams finished speaking. The new information renewed Gamble's interest in this case.

"Yeah, yeah," Gamble managed to reply. "You got plans tonight?"

"You can't be serious! The story still doesn't make any sense. We've got no witnesses. The kid survived. Maybe he got mandrakes off eBay and tried them out," Williams said.

"Indulge me. You can wait in the car while I check it out." Gamble's eyes stayed focused on his report.

"What's there to check out? It's an empty lot!" Williams protested.

"Then it won't take long at all." Gamble replied.

At half past nine—around the same time Peter McCain supposedly came the night before—Andrew Gamble arrived at 121 Mulberry Road. He wanted to see whether the house would magically appear at the same time as the night before.

No sign of Williams. Not a surprise. He waited twenty minutes, but neither his partner nor the house showed up.

Case closed.

Peter McCain had been in a psychiatric hold for a month. He had insisted he told the truth. As much as his parents wanted him home, they felt he belonged in the hospital until he stopped talking about walking mandrakes.

One day, he had trouble breathing. It grew steadily worse; his doctor ordered a chest X-ray to find out any possible blockage. The X-ray revealed a small plant growing inside Peter's lungs. The doctor promptly scheduled a surgical removal of the surprised discovery the next day.

"She wanted... to use me... to grow her... mandrake daughter... a boy... friend!" Peter struggled to say as he lay in the prep room before his surgery.

"We hear you. Now, you're gonna sleep a bit while we take this thing out of your lungs. Count to ten for me, okay, Peter?" the anaesthetist gave the other nurse a wink. Most of the hospital staff knew about Peter's mandrake story by now. Once in a while someone ingested a seed and something grew in that person's stomach. The same could happen to the lungs when someone inhaled a seed too.

Just before he fell asleep, he saw Maribel again. Still wearing her soiled apron, she peered through the curtains surrounding his hospital bed.

"Hm...It smells like gingerbread in here!" a nurse exclaimed.

The Mansion

By Karen Dales

re you sure about this?" asked Aaron.

"I'll be fine," replied Rachel. She stood with her hand on the massive wood lined glass door as Aaron, her head chef, and the rest of the closing staff filed out the door after another busy night. "I have a tonne of paperwork to catch up on. If I don't send out the monthly report tonight, you'll have to break in a new General Manager," she laughed.

Aaron grimaced, clearly not liking her staying late. "Just stay safe. I'll see you tomorrow evening."

Rachel placed a comforting hand on his arm, as he walked past and out into the cool Hallowe'en night air, towards his car. She noticed the concerned expressions on her employees, as they dispersed towards their vehicles or to the transit stop at the corner. Releasing a stress filled breath, she closed the heavy wooden door and turned the locks.

New to the position of General Manager of this prestigious and iconic restaurant in Toronto, Rachel was impressed by her staff's efficiency at cleaning and resetting the place after the last patrons left. Turning around, Rachel left a couple of lights on to illuminate her way, though the jack-o-lanterns beside the hostess station remained dark. The scent of their extinguished candles long since dissipated. .

Every day she came to work she was struck by the stately beauty of the Victorian mansion. Walking past elaborately decorated rooms that once were the living spaces to the original home owners, Rachel smiled at the wooden tables set for diners that would not arrive until tomorrow's lunch rush. A part of her fantasized what it would have been like to live in this home-turned-restaurant, amongst its mahogany wainscoting and intricate plastered ceiling designs. As much as possible, the original architecture and design was kept save for the modern necessities required to run the establishment.

On a last moment's desire, Rachel turned away from the wide, dark wood staircase lined with darkened craft pumpkins and headed towards the deserted kitchen. If she was going to stay late, she would need something to keep her awake. Passing through the double doors, Rachel flipped the switch on the wall next to the doors. Bright, modern daylight flooded the pristine silver and white kitchen.

The steel carafe would be absent of coffee grounds and water. A gallon of coffee would be too much at this late hour. Instead, Rachel walked over to the tea rack, pulled out a bag of her favourite, and grabbed a black plastic serving tray, a silver tea pot and white mug from the shelving housing all the serving plates and accoutrements. The hot water dispensary would still be on, and placing the tray on the prep table, with the mug resting on it, Rachel walked around the table to fill the pot.

Steam filled the air, as hot water rose in the pot's depths. Satisfied, Rachel placed the tea bag to steep and turned around to…

Rachel frowned. The ceramic mug no longer sat on the prep table, though the tray had not moved. Gazing around the kitchen, she found it on the counter next to the dishwashing station. Sure that she had not placed it there, she walked over and grabbed it with her free hand, placed it on the tray with the pot and flipped off the lights before exiting the kitchen. Surprised at her apparent absentmindedness, she wondered if she should have made a strong pot of coffee instead.

The Mansion

In the quiet of the place, she carried the tea and mug up the two flights of stairs to the third floor where the office and storage room resided. Though the restaurant had been around for decades, it had only been within the last decade that the third floor had been renovated. It did not make any sense to Rachel why such a prosperous and well established eatery would take so long to complete the changes.

She did like the historic touch of keeping photos of the original home owners and blurbs of the mansion's history on the wall of the first set of stairs to the second floor where the bar, other dining rooms and bathrooms resided. The photo of the lady of the mansion, flanked by her maid, and a little boy in dark shorts held up by suspenders caught her eye. Carefully balancing the tray, Rachel straightened the crooked photo with a smile. What it would have been like to have lived there. Then again, according to the write-up next to the framed photo, it seemed the three did not have as good as a life as she would have thought. Frowning slightly, she continued up to the second floor.

A flash of light out of the corner of her eye, by the bar caught her attention, as she headed to the third floor. A bulb must have blown, she surmised, and then dismissed the thought. How could a light bulb blow when all the lights were turned off? Taking a deep cleansing breath, Rachel dismissed the notion of what she thought she saw as a figment of her tired mind. Maybe a shot of something stronger in her tea would be in order.

Arriving at the third floor, Rachel managed to open the doors near the stairs without spilling any tea, and walked in. She halted several steps in. The lights had been off when she went to let everyone go home. Now they were all ablaze. Placing her pot and mug on her desk, she chalked it up to forgetfulness.

She sat down at her desk and shook the mouse to awaken the computer before pouring a mug of tea. The monitor flickered as the computer fan whirred to life. Cupping her drink, Rachel absentmindedly blew across the brown liquid, making the steam rise sideways for a moment. She took a cautious sip and opened the report she needed to work on. Procrastination tended to mar her ability to keep on track with work. Then again, she did not like the paperwork aspect of her job. People, she loved. She had so much fun having the children from the neighbourhood come around for sweet treats specially made by Aaron. Hallowe'en had always been her favourite holiday. Tea set beside her, she focused on her work she hoped to finish before morning.

Fingers flying on the keyboard, her attention kept on the monitor as she reached for the mug and grasped air. Surprised that she missed, she turned her gaze.

Gone!

Rolling her chair back, she looked on the floor beside the desk. Maybe she had accidentally knocked it onto the hard wood and had not noticed, but there was no dark water pooling on the floor. She did not recall finishing the mug's contents. Regardless, she bent over to see if it had rolled under the desk.

A loud explosion startled her, causing Rachel to smack her head on the underside of the desk. Heart pounding, she did not move. Eyes wide at the unexpected sound, she carefully sat up and gazed around for the source of the bang.

Nothing.

Except for the mug sitting upside-down in the far corner of the room in front of the filing cabinet.

She could not figure out how it got there, let alone without leaving a trail of liquid. Rising from her seat, Rachel cautiously approached the mug and bent down to retrieve it. Scalding hot tea, released from its confines, created a puddle where once stood the mug. Shocked at the impossibility, her hand released the cool cup. It shattered as it impacted the floor.

Her mind balked at what she had witnessed, and she backed away from the shattered remains mixed with tepid tea. The only rational thought that came to mind propelled her into motion to find towels to clean the mess. Turning around, she walked further into the large room, towards the stainless steel racks that contained the cardboard boxes that stored the restaurant's cleaning supplies, extra tableware and seasonal decorations.

She unwrapped a spool of paper towel and headed back to the bizarre mess. Careful not to cut herself on the sharp edges, Rachel cleaned up, placing the debris in the waste paper bin by the desk. Hands covered in cooling tea, she picked the basket up and headed downstairs to the second floor to dispose of the contents.

Heartbeat returned to normal, she dismissed the incident. She did not remember taking the mug across the room or turning it upside down on the floor. The bang must have come from outside. Nevertheless, she hugged the bin to her chest, as she descended the stairs and walked into the bar area. She flipped the light switch on the wall behind the bar. Reassuring yellow brilliance flooded the area and she sighed. The large waste bin under the bar would be perfect to dump the mess, and then she could get back to work.

The sound of destroyed cup hitting plastic mingled with the high pitched giggle of a child.

Rachel dropped her bin into the other and spun around to look towards the stairs. A shadow seemed to settle on the stairs to the third floor, but upon shaking her head, the blur disappeared.

Hands shaking, she pressed her wrist against her forehead. *I must be more tired than I thought.*

Placing the office garbage bin onto the floor, Rachel went to the women's washroom to clean up, flicking on the light as she entered. Was that mist coalescing by the sinks? She shook her head to clear it and with it the mist. Heels clicking across tile, she turned on the faucet to wash her hands and gazed at her tired reflection. The warm water cascaded over her hands. She really needed to get back to work. The report may be done almost done, but it still had to be emailed off and next week's schedule had to be written up.

The door to the empty stall behind her quietly opened.

Frozen at the sight in the mirror, Rachel did not notice the water freezing her hands.

The toilet flushed.

Heart in her throat, Rachel fled the bathroom without turning off the lights or the faucet. She slammed the bathroom door closed behind her before leaning her back against the wooden barrier. Her mind played games. She could almost imagine hearing footfalls on the other side of the door.

Moving away, she walked on unsteady legs towards the bar. She needed something stronger than tea to motivate her. The bottle of Jack called and she grabbed a half-pint tumbler from the wrack of clean glasses below the bar, cracked the bottle and poured two fingers of the amber liquid. She downed the burning drink.

A giggle titillated her ears.

Rachel closed her eyes and set the glass down. "This isn't real."

A tug on her black skirt snapped her eyes open.

Rats. It must be rats.

But how can rats reach up past her knee to the hem of her skirt?

She glanced down to see what her skirt had gotten caught on.

Nothing.

A shiver ran up her spine, and the unwarranted fear soaked her brow. She poured more whiskey into her glass and chugged it back. The burning made more sense than her rampant and exhausted imagination. The lightness and warmth from the alcohol spread through her body, relaxing her muscles and alleviated anxiety.

It must be a prank, she rationalised, as she leaned on the bar and held her head in her hand. It was not unheard of. Staff at her other service jobs loved to monkeyshine. Why not here, especially on Hallowe'en? Except that no one wanted to stay late for closing. More often than naught, her employees would set their availability for early shifts, leaving closing for the new hires. If they lasted more than a few days they would change their availability, thus the headache that ensued every week to figure out the work schedule.

Leaving the empty tumbler on the bar, she headed back towards the stairs that would take her back to her overdue work.

The sound of porcelain breaking halted Rachel's foot from landing on the stair.

Eyes wide, her first instinct was that an intruder had infiltrated the restaurant. The sound originated from one of the darkened dining rooms off to the side of the bar. No one could have entered the second floor without Rachel noticing. Taking a shuddering breath, she walked towards the room, each step ponderous, guided by a thundering heart.

The Mansion

A second crash broke the silence, halting her in her tracks by the entrance to the room. Diffuse light filtered in from the large windows adjacent to the ornamental ancient fireplace, illuminating the room in a soft glow. The sight of two tables missing a couple of bread plates prompted Rachel to flip on the light switch with a trembling hand.

There, across the room, on the floor by the wall, lay the white remnants of what used to be plates. Swallowing her rising terror, Rachel decided not to clean up the mess.

The sound of a child's giggle spun her around to see a blurred form race down the stairs.

A child? Who would have left their child here unnoticed? But it made a better reason for the chaos than the tricks of her imagination. Indignation washed away fear and she marched down the stairs, intent to stop him from breaking more items. Once she caught him, she would call the police. Hopefully, afterwards, she would be able to finish her work uninterrupted.

Rachel halted at the bottom of the stairs and looked around. No sight or sound of the child. Determined, she turned to the left to hunt down the miscreant through the different dining rooms. Halfway over to the first room, the sound of a child's footfalls on the stairs resonated through the main floor.

The little pest had run back upstairs.

Returning to the front entrance, Rachel halted in her tracks, eyes wide and mouth dry. There, hanging from a noose connected to the balustrade lining the oval opening to the second floor, a translucent woman in nineteenth century dress swayed. Rachel recognised the woman as the maid who had committed suicide by hanging herself from the second floor after her lady's passing.

Heart fluttering, Rachel could only watch as the apparition faded away to the sound of invisible footpads on the stairs. A tug on her blouse pulled her attention from the stairs to the Lady's diaphanous little boy from the photograph, who had died young by falling down the stairs. He now stood beside her.

"Play with me," said the boy, gazing up at her.

Heart throbbing between her ears, the room and the creature receded to blackness.

Cheryl, the opening manager, unlocked the front doors to the mansion to let the first crew in. It always took some time to prepare for the lunch rush. Entering the vestibule, a frown pulled on her lips. The number of lights on was against policy. Rachel knew that and should have shut them off when she left. Cheryl's annoyance turned to alarm at the sight of Rachel unconscious on the floor near the stairs. She and the two other opening crew ran to their crumpled general manager.

"Rachel!" cried Cheryl, as she knelt by her boss. She felt for a pulse.

Nothing.

"What is it?" asked Garth, a tremor in his voice.

Cheryl fell backwards to sit hard on the floor, eyes wide in shock.

Morris knelt down next to the prone figure, his fingers finding the jugular and nothing else. "Holy shit!" he exclaimed, backing away.

"Dead?" asked Garth, his jaw dropping. "Rachel's *dead?*"

The three glanced at each other, tears threatening to spill as tremors shook their forms.

A sound of footfalls raced down the stairs towards them and Rachel's cold corpse, and then past them towards one of the darkened dining rooms. The opening crew turned towards the disembodied sound then back to each other, terror draining their features.

A little boy's giggle filled the entrance.

Followed by Rachel's laughter.

Two Trees

By Vanessa C. Hawkins

A lot of people don't know the significance of the two trees. Nowadays, they walk on by during a hot day, take a rest beneath their shade while having a drink from a canteen, and look over at the cemetery beyond. No one realises that my Mama and Daddy, long since festered away, are beneath their feet.

From inside the cemetery, I see them every night, my calloused hands bracing the iron bars of the bone yard. People don't see me watching them, but sometimes when the day ends they do. I never thought I'd be left to guard them for an eternity.

Mama named me Margaret. She used to tell me it meant pearl, and Daddy said I was as pretty as one, but I didn't believe him. We lived in Shantytown where if pearls were found, they were given to the richer folk who came down in the summers to enjoy the fresh breeze blown off from the Bay of Fundy. When I was younger, I would watch the tide. You could throw a rock a kilometre, and depending on the time of day it may or may not hit the water. I heard Daddy say once that we had the highest tides in the whole wide world.

"Get away from there, Margaret. You wanna be mauled by the merfolk?"

I looked up from the between the boats moored at the wharf, listening to Daddy chuckle as the vessels bobbed up and down behind him. He had been collecting old ropes to use for netting, anything that could be salvaged and reused. Beads of sweat formed on his forehead.

"Merfolk aren't real," I protested, stepping back anyway. The sun was brilliant in my eyes, and I squinted to see. My daddy stood on the St. Andrews wharf, nothing but a silhouette.

"Sure are," he said without the amused hitch in his voice that usually accompanied his candor. "S'why we gotta feed 'em." He passed me the ropes, and then bent down to look between the boats. I was supposed to be watching out for the Wharfinger, making sure he didn't notice what we were doing. Instead, I found myself preoccupied.

"What if we don't feed them?" I had taken more than a few steps away from the edge of the wharf now.

"Then they gets *really* hungry."

I looked over my shoulder as Daddy bent to retrieve another piece of rope. Though the sea ebbed away into low tide, I could see the waves rolling into white foam on the horizon, making it look like there were creatures in the water. With the sun behind me, I was sure I saw the great tails of merfolk sparkling in the Bay of Fundy, open maws slobbering and hungry for little girls like me.

I squeezed the sea-sodden ropes in my hands until the rockweed bladders entwined within popped and oozed over my fingers. The salty breeze whipping at my soiled linen shift stung my eyes, so I closed them, forgetting my duty as watchman.

"You aren't paying any attention, Margaret," I heard my Daddy grumble before he tossed a bunch of rope over my shoulders. I almost collapsed from the weight of them, imagining a great big sea snake hissing in my ears as it squeezed me to death and dragged me down under.

"Let's get goin' home before Mama gets irate."

Two Trees

The seawater soaked through my clothes and ran in rivulets down my sides to the back of my knees. Still, I nodded. I was leaving footprints in the dirt the whole way home, smelling the pungent odor of the Bay. An old bundle of potato cloth was tangled within the ropes, and I vaguely wondered if merfolk shed their scales like snakes did.

We walked back to Shantytown, the Bay disappearing behind the ramshackle homes where all the living poor resided. Mama had a chowder ready for us when we arrived. She was all excited to have had the milk to make it, saying how the lady at the house she cleaned had given it to her for getting the wine stain out of her good handkerchief. I didn't listen much as she prattled on. Instead, I'd been thinking of what Daddy had said and the severity in which he'd said it.

"Margaret Stewart, look at you! You look like a bundle of sea trash," she said, finally taking notice of me.

"Leave 'er be, Maria. She was helpin' me at the docks."

I watched Daddy hang his hat next to the basin Mama washed the dishes in. We had set the ropes outside. Flies already buzzed around them, sometimes finding their way into the house to bother our dinner.

"She can wash up after supper. We're both hungrier than bears in spring."

It may have been true for Daddy, but it sure wasn't for me. Despite the long day of walking and heaving old wet ropes, I didn't want any of Mama's fish chowder. Not after smelling the burst rockweed and dank slime of the Bay all day.

I couldn't say that though, else I was bound to get a hidin'. So, instead, I sat at the table in my soiled linen shift and said my prayers, contemplating monsters as I forced down Mama's well-earned seafood chowder.

I had heard of mermaids before. On the really nice boats, they were there at the prow with their bare chests, sweating with seawater. Mama had told me that they gave the sailors good luck, but now I wondered why. Was it a disguise? A trick to tame the rage of the real sea monsters?

No, I thought, spooning at another chunk of mackerel floating in my bowl. Daddy was putting me on. I was twelve, too old to be believing in fairy tales and nightmares.

Still, when Daddy asked me to come outside with him to toss the garbage, I didn't wanna. He did it every night. Right beside our house, down a narrow path through a garble of trees was a cliff side. Daddy would pitch the trash over the side of the rocks by our house and I'd watch the hungry tide sweep it into the Bay until he'd yell back to me to get going.

Though I usually liked getting out the house for a walk before bedtime, I made extra sure my feet were planted on the ground as I made my way to the cliff. The moon shone big and swollen, so it was easy to see my Daddy's back as he hauled the heft of trash over one shoulder. Everyone always pitched their trash in the Bay. The high tides swept it away nice and clean, though sometimes I saw bundles of old potato cloth when the tide was out.

We could hear the waves hushing the night to be silent as they crashed against the cliffs. I could still taste Mama's chowder in my mouth, and the briny flavour of mackerel lingered on my tongue.

"Gotta feed the tide," Daddy said, stopping just short of where the bank collapsed. I skulked up behind him, wringing my hands together as he hurled the burlap sack over the side.

We didn't have much for trash. We didn't have much to begin with, so what we threw away was limited. But still, as I watched as the Bay tide swallowed it up, I swore that I heard growls between the crash of waves.

"Daddy, wait for me!" I called, horrified that he'd left without me.

Normally, I would watch as the Bay of Fundy carried away our trash. After then, I didn't anymore. Not even when the other kids went down to the shore to go beach combing. Instead, I sat on the old red rocks, watching as they picked up debris and stomped on the crabs that would come running out from underneath. Unlike the other kids, I knew that hours before when the tide was high, there might have been monsters waiting beneath the bundles of seaweed and the old discarded potato cloth, instead of six-legged crustaceans.

"Stay in your room, child."

Two Trees

My Daddy's voice.

In the kitchen, our paraffin lamp glowed dimly among the shadows. The moon had hidden behind the clouds. The air smelled of the sea, curiously mingled with copper.

I didn't remember getting up, but thought I must have gotten out of bed to relieve myself. The vague shapes from inside our shack were forming in the corners of my eyes, and as I tried to peer past the shadows in the kitchen to the front door, I heard a painful scream from Mama, and gasped.

"Get back to bed!" she screamed, drawing out the last vowel in a squeal of manic pain. I didn't dare protest. Instead, I leapt over the threshold that separated the kitchen from where I slept and closed the door.

We lived in a small shack, nothing but the bare necessities. Usually, Mama and Daddy and I slept in the same room off the kitchen. When I jumped into the homey mattress that was my bed, I could hear Daddy out in the kitchen. The muffled sounds of furniture scraping along the dirt floor as stifled moans and groans resounded in our little house.

Beneath the covers, terrified, I tucked the blankets up over my head, trying to block the sounds out. Mama breathed hard, Daddy grumbling. After a few short moments, I finally managed the courage to defy Mama's orders and peer over the headboard of my slight little bed and into a chink in the wall.

Blood pooled on our dirt floor. I stifled a scream, ducking back down to cram my head into my pillow.

Daddy would butcher pigs, sometimes chickens. I've seen things die up at the farms, when he had to go to work there. Curious, I had wanted to watch as those animals had their heads cut off. Sick fascination had led to disgust; disgust, eventually to disappointment. This reminded me of those times, and despite my Mama's warning that I mind my own and stay inside the room, my morbid interest drew me back to that slit in the wall.

Something squirmed in Daddy's hands right before it began to wail.

"Daddy? Is something the matter?" I asked, playing dumb.

Daddy didn't know it, but I saw him look towards the door to our bedroom. He had his hand over a babe's mouth, and the sound of crying stopped.

"Ain't nothing, Margaret. Your Mama's just sick. Go back to bed."

Mama lay on the kitchen table with her legs apart, a leather strap in her mouth, her teeth clenching down hard on it as she struggled to breathe.

"Is she alright?" The blood on the table and the floor gleamed in the lamplight.

"S'fine. I gotta take the trash out. Forgot to at supper. Go to bed, Margaret."

I didn't know until much later, but back then, when there were unwanted children, it wasn't uncommon for them to be wrapped up in potato cloth and thrown into the sea. It wasn't just our house that had done it.

At the time, I didn't understand what I had seen.

Daddy left our house, the babe in his hands swaddled carefully in that old potato cloth. His thick, calloused palm muffled the babe's cries. He shut the door behind him.

I turned back around, settled beneath the blankets, and fell asleep to the sound of her blood dripping on the kitchen floor.

In the morning, they told me it had all been a dream. That there hadn't been a babe at all.

"But you said Mama was sick. I heard crying!"

Daddy spooned at the bowl of beans Mama had heated for breakfast. He shook his head, looking up at me from beneath his severe slope of forehead. Beyond the window, a pall of gray clouds cloaked the sky. The air was chilly.

Mama said, "I ain't gonna tell you anymore stories, Margaret, if they're givin' you nightmares."

Her face was gaunt and pale, her body deflated like a dried-up cucumber. She sat at the stove by the fire, boiling Daddy's old socks clean. The entire shack smelled of beans, mackerel, and damp feet. The faint smell of copper, too. The blood on the floor was gone.

"If it was all just a dream, then why you so tired? You look like you were up all night, Mama. You look *sick*."

"You best take her to church on the way to the docks," she told Daddy, then narrowed her eyes at me. "Pray away that sinful imagination."

Mama looked back to the fire. The cool wind was coming from off the water this morning, but she was wrapped up in her winter blanket *and* her summer shawl.

I didn't believe I could have imagined it all up, but Mama and Daddy got angry when I mentioned it again. Daddy took me to church later in the day, just like Mama said he should.

Days after, I started coming back out to the sea when Daddy took the trash out, started believing' that my mind had some evil in it. Even when I continued seein' the merfolk in the water, snarling under the waves, I'd say to myself: *They aren't real. A figment of my vile imagination.*

Every day, the continuous roar of the sea against the cliff side worked upon my imagination so that I heard snarls, malevolent sighs, hissing. Soon, I was certain I heard a babe's cries echoing among them from the Bay.

I fancied the babe as my little sister. *Pearl,* I called her, because she ought to be as pretty as one.

Mama and Daddy, you drowned her in the Bay of Fundy.

Mama's voice protested in my mind: *No, we did not. How could you even dare think we'd do such a thing? After all we do to take care of you?*

I stared at the water, listening to my baby sister's wails, hoping that mermaids had found her, taken her to some underwater kingdom away from all the garbage we threw in the sea. There, she could live out her days in happiness. I wanted to join her, throw myself from the wharf and see where the sea took me. I understood, however, that I'd only sink, become some waterlogged body buried under seaweed, under garbage and potato cloth, an anchor hold for some rich man's boat.

Or meat for the merfolk.

There are no merfolk!

I heard Pearl crying.

There is no Pearl. It was a dream!

When Daddy went to throw out the trash, I saw her ghost, trapped within the waves every night. The merfolk taunted her, dragged her beneath the sea to drown her again and again.

"Hurry along, Margaret," my Daddy said as he began walking back to Shantytown, hands empty from the haul of nightly trash. He must have thought my fears of the Bay were quelled, since I rejoined him on his walk to the cliff side. Instead, they grew.

Why couldn't he see it, too? Was my mind ripe with wicked fascinations? Or was he hiding from the murder he and Mama had committed?

Was I crazy? Did no one else hear the babe screaming from the sea?

At the end of the summer, I got a job at the Kennedy House. Small work. Not a bad job for a girl with a sturdy set of shoulders. Mostly, I cleaned and laundered the soiled clothes of the richer folks vacationing for the season. It was away from the seaside—as much as anything could be in St. Andrews—and enough of a distraction to keep me from thinking of Pearl.

"Did you hear what happened, Margaret?" Delilah, my coworker, asked as she scrubbed at the stains on some bedclothes. We were both down in the basement of the Kennedy House, old cobwebs and the squeak of mice keeping us company. "The Wharfinger's closed the wharf."

I looked up, staring into Delilah's dark brown eyes. She was taller than me, prettier, with a round face and sunshine in her eyes. She was older than me by two whole years, but I was certain that most of the Kennedy guests thought she was younger.

"Why?" I asked, feeling phantom fingers poking down my spine.

Delilah smiled, looking around conspiratorially. I could tell she was pleased to be the first one to relay this piece of gossip. "They found a body in the water. All mauled up and half eaten. Now everyone's sayin' the sea's haunted."

I dropped the tablecloth I was scrubbing into the basin. Water splashed over the side and onto Delilah's apron. She grimaced, tutting that I should watch what I was doing.

"What kind of body, Delilah? Tell me. Tell me now." I asked, eyes as wide as dinner plates. I held myself back from saying, *Was it a babe? A child?*

Delilah stared at me with guarded curiosity, taken aback by my sudden outburst. Bending to her work, she resumed her task with the laundry. "It was a sailor," she said after a while, stopping to wipe her forehead. "But I guess the body looked pretty bad."

She regarded me. I stared down into the washbasin, watching the tablecloth settle into the water until only a small section of it bobbed on the surface.

It reminded me of a baby's head.

"I've heard people sayin' they've heard cries though," Delilah continued, "babes in the water."

'Since when?" My voice was barely a whisper.

I watched her bite the inside of her cheek, no longer pleased to spread such gossip.

"Just heard about it, is all," Delilah continued. "In either case, the wharf is closed. All the rich folks'll be disappointed, and so I imagine they'll be taking it out on us."

I watched as she hauled her laundry from the water into a basket. "Better get this done quick," she said, walking away with the load in her arms.

I'm not crazy! Pearl really was out on the water. Thrown to the ravenous tide by my Mama and Daddy! Crying out for someone to save her. The merfolk were the ones that had killed the sailor! How else?

I went to the sea that night. Defying the Wharfinger's orders, I cut the ropes of a small skiff and went out as far as I could in hopes to save my sister. At the worst case, I thought, Pearl's ghost would rise up to drown me for not saving her, and then perhaps I could be there with her at least, and stave off the merfolk that tortured her.

The high tide and the gibbous moon kissed as my paddle split the waves. All around me, I saw them, the domes of their skulls decorated with knotted rockweed.

"I hear you, Pearl!" I screamed, watching as they crowded the skiff and tossed it teetering on the surf. From underneath, I could hear the merfolk's fists pounding at the keel. They had limbs like drywood, shards of sea-glass in their eyes. As they rose up from the water, the Bay exhaled, and fierce winds sent the skiff hurtling backwards, dropping down into the valleys of the sea.

"Pearl!" I saw her. She was bundled in the potato cloth, her forehead dry from where Daddy had kissed her. She drifted through the moonlight, cradled within the sweeping arc of the tidal waves. Serpentine tails with scabby black fins and missing scales sloshed around her. Bones stuck out from the merfolk's torsos. Barnacles burst from their thick skin, meandering around mouths crowded with shark teeth and tentacles.

"No! Leave her alone!"

The Bay inhaled, and floating upon the lung of the sea, I pierced the rushing water with my paddle. The salt on my face stung my eyes. The wind whipped at my hair and clothes. I couldn't reach her, was too far away, and in my desperation the wave transformed, moonlight illuminating its malformation.

Foam frothed at the edge of the water. Serpent eyes breached the surface. I fell back into the skiff as the Bay of Fundy reared back and closed its maw around Pearl. Her cries pierced my brain and left me feeling helpless as the surface began to equalize and the skiff settled back into place, right overtop where her body had been. The boat marked her grave like a tombstone.

I whimpered, holding my knees. The sodden ropes littering the bottom of the boat floated around me. The wind pushed the water over the edge. I heard the monsters. Was I going to be eaten alive, too? Like the sailor on the wharf?

"Leave us alone. Leave her, me, alone." I offered Pearl so many tears, and the Bay answered with the sounds of waves and merfolk voices.

At high tide, when the belly of the Bay was pregnant with monsters and the moon was full and farthest from the sun, I said my prayers and dove into its depths. I knew she was there, prisoner of the surf, and as I sunk down deep, my limbs filling with water, I swore I would find her.

The rockweed swept over me and all the discarded potato cloth and trash of the sea wrapped about my legs. Trapped, I began to drown as the seabed buried me beneath its debris. As my lungs slowly began to fill with water, I panicked, kicking as I closed my eyes, fearful that I had failed to help her. But when I opened them again, I could see the sun piercing through the

Bay. Pearl was there, above the surface, giggling from the prow of my skiff and haloed in the morning light. I reached out to her and smiled, glad that she had been freed from the merfolk, from the sea monsters that had invaded my nightmares and hers.

Leaving my body behind, I swam to the surface to join her.

August 29th, 1826 was the day they hung my parents. It cost eight shillings to build the gallows. Though the ordeal surrounding my parents was to remain quiet, the bells always tolled with every hanging, and it did so then without prejudice. Mama and Daddy hung until two o'clock in the hot afternoon. They had been there since nine in the morning. Potato cloth hoods were placed over their heads, a suitable end even though they didn't hang for Pearl.

Some wealthy old man had found my body curled up inside his anchor. I stayed in the sea fighting for Pearl until they pulled me out. Authorities deduced that I had been strangled about the neck with an old rope, the same kind Daddy used to fetch from the sea when he thought the Wharfinger wasn't looking. It had been the Wharfinger's testimony that had truly sent my folks to the gallows. If only I had been a better lookout.

Mama and Daddy hung for my death. The community of St. Andrews dragged my body from the sea and buried it in the St. Andrews bone yard, right alongside the cemetery gate. Just outside its iron bars stood the two trees.

Criminals could not be buried in the cemetery. Only the righteous and just could lay their souls to rest in sanctified church soil. I am sure there were many who had fled the courts and were buried six feet under and went straight to hell, but Mama and Daddy were not allowed to be among those in the St. Andrews Catholic cemetery. Instead, they were buried alongside it, just outside the gate and beside my headstone.

They are close by us always: Pearl and I. We walk along the cemetery together, my soul with hers, who will never see her body at rest. We don't hate them for what they did, but they suffer now beneath the ground, eternally drowning as we stand sentinel.

I wish I knew why they did it, why they threw Pearl to the

Bay like trash. They had loved me, provided for me and nurtured me like loving parents were wont to do. I remember Mama singing hymns to me, telling me tales of kings and queens. I remember Daddy telling me how someday I'd go to school and get out of Shantytown. Earn enough money to take care of them when they were old and gray.

Was our family so poor to provide love and care for Pearl as well?

Don't worry. We'll never be apart again.

Two trees. There are two trees outside the graveyard. You can see them still if you're walking down the Prince of Wales towards the shore, away from Shantytown where the poor had laboured. Those trees are the headstones of my Mama and Daddy. In the space between them, the spouses touch, feet to feet, their bones wound between the roots, hoods still over their heads. I lay within the bone yard, not very far away from them. My gravestone fell down a while ago and the grass has hidden it from those who come to pay the dead respect, but I'm still there, forever with Pearl, whose body will never be put to rest.

Stag and Storm

By Sara C. Walker

This story takes place in Central Ontario at the time of
Hurricane Hazel.

azel Cormorant's little cottage was filled with hearts in jars: frog hearts, mice hearts, pig hearts, squirrel hearts, raven hearts. If it crossed her path, she took its heart and preserved it in a washed-out pickle jar just as her father had taught her. Hearts were key to the survival of a species. Weak hearts made for short lives.

Long after her father's death, Hazel lived her life sowing seeds, gathering herbs, and putting hearts in jars as she saw fit, until the day she met the one heart she couldn't have.

One night in October, classical music played from a hand-crank radio as the day's rain continued to patter on the roof. Hazel Cormorant rocked in her chair while reading an old science journal from the University of Toronto, reminiscing of the days when she first saw her father's name in print. How easy to be published back then. He made it seem so natural.

Hazel's cottage rested in the heart of Central Ontario, deep in the woods. The nearest post office and general store were ten miles away, and it took her a good deal longer to get there ever since the horse died. Nowadays, when she had to do business at these establishments, she would set out before dawn and drag the mule along to do the carrying. The mule had few years left, which meant Hazel would soon have to buy a new horse or a new mule. She had no intention of leaving this little cottage until her work was complete. Mule or no mule.

A weather bulletin interrupted the soft notes of Chopin. Her ears perked up. The announcer cited the hurricane that had made landfall earlier in the day:

"The intensity of this storm has decreased to the point where it should no longer be classified as a hurricane. This weakening storm will continue to push northward, passing east of Toronto before midnight. The main rainfall associated with it should end shortly thereafter, with occasional light rain occurring throughout the night. Winds will increase slightly to forty-five to fifty miles per hour until midnight, then slowly decrease throughout the remainder..."

Static drowned out the reporter's voice. Hazel stood up and switched off the radio.

She'd just settled back into her rocking chair, when there sounded a knock at the door. It startled her. She never had visitors.

She went to the door and opened it. A man of measurable size stood on the doorstep. The kind of man that would have a big heart. She immediately wondered at its strength.

He looked about forty, give or take a few years, and he almost twice her size. Hazel took after her mother's hearty Dutch heritage, people built like tree trunks. Still, as limber and as strong as she might be in her old age, she knew to be cautious with strangers.

"Madam," he said. "I require shelter until the storm passes."

She raised an eyebrow. "Storm?"

His nostrils flared. "You don't sense its approach? You didn't notice the absence of birdsong from the trees or bird-flight from the sky today?"

She had, in fact, made such observances. She'd even noticed

the rabbits scurrying for higher ground that morning. The meteorologists, however, had data that told a different story. They knew wind patterns and barometric pressure on a scale that animal instinct could not possibly comprehend.

The cottage was one room, except for the pantry and the bathroom, so it would be close quarters for the night. She could have told him to shelter in the chicken coop or with the mule, but chose against it. Something intelligent gleamed in his warm brown eyes that reminded her of the way her father looked at her that time she cut herself with the axe. For once, his eyes were not glued to his notes or his microscope.

It had been some time since she'd fed and cared for another human, but she expected she could remember how.

"You may shelter here," she said. She had to clear her throat twice before she could speak, and even then, her voice pitched like a squeaky hinge.

He nodded his gratitude as he crossed the threshold.

"Paul Koenig," he said. His voice was deep but soft, putting her in mind of strong earthy elements like fat, spongy moss.

"Hazel Cormorant," she replied.

Paul noticed the jars around the room, his eyes following the rows of shelves. The light from the oil lamps flickered as the air settled. Paul flared his nostrils again. Perhaps he was not familiar with the scent of formaldehyde. To Hazel, it smelled like home and she preferred it to the wet musk rolling off the man.

"Biologist," she said, pre-empting his query. "My father's work, until I assumed it."

He gave a nod in response. Were his lips pressed tight? Or was she imagining it?

He nodded at the rain dripping into a pail behind the rocking chair. "Will this place hold up to the storm?"

Hazel looked to the ceiling. "It's not as it once was," she said, shrugging, annoyed he still believed a storm approached.

Paul had to duck his head when he passed through the doorway, and now he dwarfed the small chesterfield. He removed the sack strapped across his chest, set it by the door, and shed his deerskin jacket—a nice one with thick wool on the inside. His shirts were dry. He bent over and went to work removing his wet boots.

He was well-groomed with a recent haircut and a trimmed beard. She'd wager he was a man used to a comfortable life. His boots were new. As he retrieved fresh socks from his satchel, she noticed the sturdy canvas had a waterproof lining. He had a manner about him that said rugged wilderness man, but everything he carried could have been purchased yesterday. She found something suspicious about that.

"What brings you to my woods?" she asked.

"Following a deer trail, trying to stay ahead of the storm. Saw the smoke from your chimney," he said.

"Then we have something in common, if you're after the deer. Just recently got myself a doe. Enough to eat for the winter."

He responded with a grunt, then laid his wet socks overtop his boots and set both items to dry next to the wood stove. A hunter's socks should be worn, the wool flattened and stretched and darned. His pair appeared to be fresh off a set of knitting needles.

Hazel went to the larder and took her time selecting packed canning jars and a bundle of dried meat.

"You don't mind stew, do you?" she asked as she returned to the main room, her arms laden with a pot and provisions.

"Not at all," he said. "But I insist on making a contribution." His voice carried a tone of authority, one that assumed compliance and made Hazel's spine twitch. Just what gave him the right to come into her cottage and order her around? Was this the thanks she got for allowing him to enter her home after he'd asked—

But he *had not* asked. Not exactly.

I require shelter until the storm passes. Those had been his exact words. Not a request, but a…

Command.

Hazel frowned.

He retrieved a cloth bundle from his satchel and opened it to reveal wild herbs and mushrooms. The edible kinds.

She accepted his provision, by gesturing for him to take over making the stew. As she stirred up the coals and added wood to the cook stove, she silently reproved herself for being so quick to hand over her wooden spoon. Years of self-imposed isolation had turned her into a coward.

"My condolences on your father," he said.

Hazel stiffened. Then, she remembered telling him that she'd assumed her father's work. She nodded her thanks, not trusting herself to speak.

The sympathetic tone in his voice made her pause. She theorized he meant no harm with his demanding attitude, but only forgot his manners from time to time, something she'd been guilty of herself.

What was this man's true purpose here? Was he after her father's work? Or did he have something more nefarious in mind? She kept an eye on his motions, while he went about preparing their supper with her sharpest kitchen knife. She might be spry for her age, but he still had the advantage of height, breadth, and weight. However, she knew where to find the axe, bow and arrows, while he did not.

The winds picked up, howling and battering against the cottage. Just as the meteorologists had predicted——increasing winds that will die away overnight. No need for Paul to keep glancing at the ceiling as though it were about to blow away.

As she made potato dumpling dough, she noticed he used plants from the woods beyond her doorstep: wild ginger, sumac bobs, and stinging nettles. She approved, but she kept getting distracted by his boots next to the stove. Barely broken in. How could he seem brand new to the forest and yet familiar with the wild edibles?

Hazel relocated the microscope, books, and piles of research papers—comparative studies of hearts, descriptions of found defects and anomalies—from the table to the plank floor, and made space for the two of them to take a proper meal.

He asked about her father and the biology. She explained his study of normal and abnormal hearts, about how valuable a helper she'd been—keeping him organized, keeping him fed, preparing his slides, cleaning up after him.

"You must have cared for him a great deal," he said.

"He was a good man," she said softly, "with a gentle heart." She gazed up at the lines of jars. Her father had been a brilliant man, his research in demand.

But then her mother died. After that, her father barely ate, barely slept, and hardly worked. The trips to the post office to send away his papers and pick up cheques came to an end along with the trips to the bank and the general store. Hazel started bringing in the eggs and the vegetables from the garden. She'd already taken over the cooking and cleaning.

But she did not have her mother's knack for finding animals with wounded hearts.

She couldn't remember at what age she'd learned that about her mother. They seemed to be always surrounded by caged animals in various states of health. Her mother would find them, bring them home, and when their shortened lives came to an end, her father would study their hearts under his microscope. They always said they made the perfect team.

In the days after her mother's death, Hazel tried to duplicate her mother's ability. She trapped the animals and presented them to her father with their hearts cut out. No easy task, it took her quite some time to build up the strength to break open a ribcage. Her father would give her a wilted smile, push the slide under the microscope, and sadly shake his head. No defect, no anomaly, no disease.

So it went, year after year. Their situation became more desperate, her father's reputation as a scientist became tenuous. Trapping and torturing the animals to produce disease and defects seemed a natural step. She'd only wanted to be a valuable assistant.

Her work was impeccable. Her father's reputation would be restored.

"It's unnatural," Paul said with a grunt. "You created those defects."

Hazel gave him a sharp look.

He wasn't wrong; the differences could be seen under the microscope. But if her father ever noticed, he never said so and he continued to be published in the journals. She pursed her lips.

Paul turned away from her. "And the empty jar?"

There were plenty of empty jars stashed around the room, mostly on the floor, but she knew the one he meant. At the very center of the longest wall, it had become the focal point of her collection.

She'd not been surprised by the question, but rather how long it had taken him to bring it up.

"Did you enjoy the stew and dumplings?" Hazel asked. "There's more. Or perhaps as the hour grows late, I'll make up a bed for you." She cleared away the bowls, the spoons and the knives, and rinsed them in the washbasin.

Yes, care and feeding came easily to her as ever.

Outside, howling wind clashed with the rain, rushed through the trees, battering the roof.

"Seems we may be having a storm after all." The scent of wet leather annoyed her. "I guess you were right."

He blinked at her, pensive but alert. "Being right was never my intention, madam. I only meant to warn."

She grit her teeth. He had such a regal, pompous attitude. "Do you predict your whole life by the pattern of birds?" she spat. "I suppose next you'll tell me it's raining because I killed a spider."

He sat a little straighter in the chair and drew in a breath that expanded his chest, but somehow his presence filled the room. He'd barely moved a muscle, but sat as though he were about to spring to his feet.

"I observe the natural order of the forest, and I assure you my decisions are sound and just." He'd not raised his voice, but she clearly heard him over the racket of the storm. He seemed to be measuring her in his words—but for what? Had she taken the animals he wanted to hunt? Didn't that make her no worse than a rival hunter?

She glanced at his socks by the woodstove. Those flawless stiches. She had to shout to be heard over the pounding rain.

"What brings you to my woods, Mr. Koenig?"

Paul rose from the chair. The storm swelled, rattling the windows. The wind blew the lights out. A cry tore loose from Hazels' mouth. Shrieking seemed to come from everywhere— the walls, the jars, the forest. The entire cottage filled with the surging crash of the storm, and then not even the screams could be heard anymore.

"I suppose that answers your question about the cottage holding up," Hazel said grimly. "Everything dies eventually. Even old cottages."

The worst of the storm had passed, leaving lashing winds and heavy rain in its wake. Hazel had relit the lamps only to find brown clumps of wet leaves dangling from a hole in the ceiling. Water and debris cascaded down the branches, falling in steady streams next to the bucket. A dark stain spread across the floorboards.

Paul *hmmm*-ed. "If the underlying structure is sound, it can be mended."

"Perhaps once. My heart's just not in it anymore."

Although all the lamps blazed once more, the cottage felt darker. A cold draught blew down from the ceiling. She went to stoke the fire in the stove.

"I'll take a look at it," he said.

Hazel gasped. "You? But the storm—"

"It's only a bit of rain," he said. "Listen. The patter slows. The wind softens."

"You could slip and fall. You're better off staying indoors." Hazel snatched up an empty bucket and placed it under the new drip.

Paul strapped on his boots and shrugged into his deerskin jacket. Hazel grabbed her rubber boots and yanked them on.

Their eyes met. She arched an eyebrow, daring him to comment on her age.

He would need someone to show him where the hammer and nails were kept, someone to show him the ladder to get up to the roof, and someone to fetch the canvas tarpaulin. He could hardly do it alone.

Certainly, no more than her father had ever worked alone.

They went out into the driving rain.

Paul Koenig had spent a lot of time in the wilderness, surviving black flies, deer ticks, and bears. He'd seen a lot of fallen trees, hollowed out logs.

He knew rot when he saw it.

More than a few shingles were needed to fix this place.

Stag and Storm

A great white oak once stood tall next to the cottage, but now rested against the roof, weary from its years of providing shade. Such trees were more common farther south; this one would have been deliberately planted.

Paul set the ladder against the cottage. Neither the wind nor the rain blew as strong as before, but this was hardly an ideal night for roof repair. Hazel brought the hammer, nails, cedar shakes and a sheet of canvas. She handed all of it over to him in a sack that Paul slung over his shoulder.

"Be careful up there. It'll be slippery."

He went up a few rungs, and she stepped forward to grip the bottom of the ladder.

The woman was not short on courage. Strong and big-boned, she could have done the repair herself when the storm passed. But her courage only extended as far as the things with which she was familiar. As soon as he challenged her, she collapsed.

He found her as easy to understand as the countryside in a thick fog before dawn. Harvesting hearts and squirrelling them away. And yet she seemed to have an intelligent mind and a strong body. So what would possess a creature to do such a thing?

Paul wrestled the limb from the hole in the roof, struggling under its weight. A stuck branch came away, lashed him across the face.

He blinked away the rain, tacked the canvas over the hole as he unfolded it, and once secured, he climbed back down the ladder. They went back inside.

Hazel sucked her teeth. "That's a nasty cut there."

Paul touched his cheek and came away with blood on his fingertips.

She leaned in to examine his face at closer proximity. "It'll scar for sure. 'Tis a shame."

She bustled about the tiny cottage and returned with a handful of towels.

"I've been scarred by worse." Paul accepted the towels and wiped rain from his head and blood from his face. "As have you, madam, with the loss of someone you loved."

She stopped with the kettle in her hand, turned her head

and examined him. "Scars on the inside never really heal, do they?"

"Sometimes the pain feels like having your heart torn from your chest."

"Hmph." She heated the kettle, and then filled a pair of cups with tea and whiskey.

Paul settled his frame against the chesterfield, his back turned to the unnerving sight of hearts in jars. Hazel sat in the rocking chair next to the wood she'd brought in from the rain and stacked beside the stove to dry, scanning her collection. Her gray hair curled in irregular clumps as it dried. Likely, she cut it herself. As with the trees and logs for her fire.

All those animals. What was her role in all this? Had she cared for the animals before they were used in the name of science? Or had it been her job to feed and to clean up after her father?

Had she ever been away from this place?

Between the whiskey that warmed from within and the freshly fed woodstove that warmed from without, he drifted to sleep.

Paul woke to birds chirping above his head. He woke with the twin scents of death and suffering filling his nostrils. He woke with Hazel Cormorant's wrinkled face hovering over him.

The sight of her startled him.

"You *are* awake," she said.

She leaned away.

He exhaled a gust of breath. "Yes. Quite."

They sat down to break the night's fast with eggs and mushrooms and tea made from leaves and flowers Hazel had dried herself. It was not his usual fare—nothing about this place was usual—but it slaked his appetite.

"I believe you were going to tell me about the special jar," he said. He spoke slowly, chose his words carefully—he always did—and kept his tone light. Being of large size, he found a gentle approach always best.

She remembered. The tale she told was this:

She'd been out in the woods one October day before her

father died, foraging puffballs for their breakfast, when she saw him standing there, proud and tall, wearing his grand antlers like a regal forest crown: the largest stag she'd ever seen.

"When our eyes met on that cold autumn morn, he huffed, sending twin plumes of steam from his nostrils, and I knew then I must have his heart."

It had been the one animal her mother had never been able to find defective.

Yet, there she stood with no more than a kitchen knife. He turned his head, as if looking behind her, and then sauntered away with nary a sound over the mist-covered ground.

For days and weeks, she returned to the woods with her bow and arrow, hunting that king of the forest, needing its heart.

"Day and night, year after year, I filled other jars, but the empty jar called out, taunting me. Without the stag, my collection was forever incomplete."

She went to the jar and ran a finger across the glass. "Every day I clear away the dust, polish up a shine, knowing the day will soon come when it will be empty no more."

She sucked her top lip against her teeth between her words, and her eyes suggested she saw only the events of that autumn morn. That she went back to that day often.

"Nothing else for that jar?" he asked.

"I've not been interested in anything else."

"Ever see the stag again?"

She crossed the room and sat in the rocking chair. "Oh, of course I did. Many times. But arrows missed the mark. The most recent time I saw him—just a few weeks ago—with a doe and a fawn. I fired my arrows—for I never leave the house without them now—and I missed the stag. I missed the fawn, too, when it took off in a panic. But I got the doe. Perhaps she'd meant to give the fawn time to run." Hazel shrugged a shoulder. "Not the heart I wanted, but at least I will have plenty to eat this winter."

Her eyes became unfocussed, far away, her voice soft, a whispered promise. "How I wish I'd got the stag instead."

Paul's leg muscles urged him to move. His mouth went dry. He stood up and thanked her for her hospitality. He gathered his things.

Hazel sat back with a twitch. She blinked, but her eyes did not clear the sight of Paul packing up to leave.

"You're not leaving, are you?" She didn't mean to sound quite as alarmed as she felt. *Foolish, Hazel.*

He buckled up the fancy canvas bag and hung it over his shoulder.

A red line traced its way from the corner of his right eye, down to his chin, then cut through his beard, where he'd been slashed by a tree branch while tacking the canvas in place. The skin welled-up, swollen and lumpy. Destined to scar.

"You're wounded. I have a salve for your face," she said. "I could care for you while you heal."

They stared at each other. Her pulse quickened. He exhaled through his nose. His eyes shifted to the wall of jars.

He reached for the door.

"But—" The word burst forth with enough force to stop him and turn him around, and as soon he did, the words died in her mouth.

He turned away and exited the cottage, the door closing behind him with nary a sound.

Hazel let out a gasp, as the door shut. He was gone. She blinked as if her eyes played tricks on her, as if he were really there, but she couldn't see him. Without Paul's presence, the cottage seemed bigger. Emptier.

She collapsed onto the chesterfield. In the days following her father's death, she hadn't known what to do with herself, she'd felt lost in her own home.

Now, she felt lost again.

His scent lingered on the chesterfield—moss and rain and that strong wet musk. He smelled like a man. He smelled like a—

Hazel's skin tingled.

She went to the place where she kept her axe and her bow and arrows, and went after the man.

Stag and Storm

Hazel knew the deer paths well. She'd wandered them every day since that October morning long ago. He hadn't gotten very far. She spotted him on the trail ahead of her.

He looked back over his shoulder, swivelling his head as though the antlers' weight meant nothing to him.

The stag stopped. He turned around.

Hazel gasped.

Her stag had acquired a red, ragged scar from his right eye down to his jawbone.

She nocked an arrow and drew back the line, a shot she'd taken many times before. Aim for the chest—the cavity with the most organs. Watch for the ribs to expand on inhale. As she sighted down the arrow, something happened: the stag became a man. It became Paul.

She lowered the bow and blinked her aged eyes. Man. Deer. She raised the bow, but again saw the man, so she threw the bow aside, and lifted the axe from where she'd cinched it into her belt.

As she crept, closing the gap between them, the stag remained a stag. Mighty and proud. Watching her with his intelligent eyes.

An animal's eyes didn't bother her. Hazel had long ago learned to ignore them. She raised the axe and swung. He met the axe handle with his majestic crown, easily knocking it from her hands.

No matter. She'd torn open enough ribcages by now that she knew exactly what to do—where to put her fingers, how much pressure to apply.

As if he interpreted the gleam in her eyes, he brought his antlers down again as Hazel lunged, hands reaching for his ribcage.

Images of him ran together. Her old eyes would not see true. Was she looking at man or beast? Both. Neither.

"You," she gasped. "How can it be you?" A bark of laughter escaped her lips pressed tight against the pain. "I served you venison."

"No, madam. You did not."

Then she remembered: she'd left the stew preparations to him. Her aged tongue hadn't known the difference.

Oh, but how she admired his sly intelligence.

"Tell me, Paul, was this the ending you intended all along? Was this the reason you showed up on my doorstep? Because I put hearts in jars? Tell me."

She blinked and he faded to beast. She blinked again and he became the man.

His nostrils flared as though he found her repugnant. "Madam, you are a black decay slowly destroying the heartwood of my forest."

Considered himself the king of the forest and all that inhabited it, did he? Hazel had always thought the forest *her own*.

"You are the disease, the anomaly, the defect," he said.

She'd not been prepared for the pain.

The point of the antler slid up through her belly, following its curved nature, but when it pierced her heart—*oh*. That surprised her.

The antler slid away and Hazel fell to the ground.

Her breath became sharply painful. Sensation faded from her limbs. High above the treetops, large birds circled the sky, their dark shapes only just visible through autumn's bare branches.

Hearts were key to the survival of the species.

"I wanted your heart," she said. "From the moment I saw you, I wanted your heart."

Those warm brown eyes went sad again, and in that moment, she understood. The doe. His mate. The knowledge came too late, and it wasn't what she'd expected, but she suddenly knew she had his heart. Just not the way she'd wanted.

He turned away from her for the final time, leaving her body to cool on the mossy ground, leaving her to decay. He drifted away, fading into the autumn mist.

The Sound of Passing Traffic

By Joe Powers

This isn't going to end well."

Lucas stood in the middle of the road with his hands balled into fists and a scowl on his face. He glared at his rusted blue Ford Taurus, mired at a severe angle in the ditch. The right front tire had sunk nearly out of sight, and no matter how much he had cursed or revved the engine, the car remained firmly lodged.

He found a grassy patch on the far side of the road, knelt down, and scraped away some of the mud from his shoes and pant legs. He stood up and glanced around in despair. How long had it been since he'd passed any sign of civilization? He thought maybe an hour or more since he'd left the highway and turned onto the rutted goat trail he was now stranded on.

He'd gotten directions from the attendant at the gas station in Murdochville, who had said the shortcut could shave several hours off his drive.

"It's gotta be two hundred kilometers or more," the guy had told him in broken English. "You don't wanna do that though."

"What do I want to do?" Lucas asked.

The guy jabbed his finger at a map on the counter. "You take the Route du Lac-Sainte-Anne, there's an old road—right here, see? That goes right to the 299. You do that, you'll cut your trip in half, easy."

Now, as he flipped up his collar against the rain, he regretted the shortcut. How badly did he want to see Gaspesie National Park? The allure of Appalachian Mountains and a caribou herd had all but vanished.

On top of his predicament was the inexplicable feeling of being watched. There was no logical explanation for it, but the sensation of unseen eyes following him was unmistakable. It was a helpless feeling that unnerved him, and he cursed the creepy isolation, as he struggled to maintain his composure.

His cellphone was useless. Reception had been spotty for a while, and now there were no bars on the screen. There was no way to figure out where he was with the GPS, pull up a map of the area, or even try to make an emergency call. Disgusted, he jammed the phone into his pocket. He closed his eyes and forced himself to calm down. A full-blown panic would only make matters worse. It occurred to him how reliant the average person is on technology, and how utterly lost those same people generally were when deprived of these conveniences. Given the circumstances he was forced to admit this applied to him, too.

Aside from a perfect stranger, who barely spoke English, nobody knew where he was. He had no way to contact the outside world. It might be days, or even longer, before anyone happened to travel down this road and stumble upon him. Exposed to the harsh elements with no food or water, he could die in a short time. He had never been in the wilds of Northern Quebec, but forests everywhere were filled with all sorts of dangers. Bears, wolves, and moose all lived in places like this. What about wolverines? Lucas didn't know about that, but he thought there might also be snakes and stinging insects to contend with, to say nothing of the various dangerous and even poisonous plants. The more he thought about it, the more convinced he was of what a perilous place the forest could be.

"You're freaking yourself out over nothing. Stop it." The sound of his voice calmed him a bit, but he couldn't shake the feeling of being watched.

The rain had progressed to a steady drizzle which drove him to seek shelter. He climbed inside the car, rolled the window down a crack, and lit a cigarette. The radio had gone silent. He fiddled with the controls, trying to find a station, but soon gave up.

A quick, furtive movement at the edge of his vision caught his eye, and he looked up. He stared off in the direction from which he'd seen it, but could make nothing out in the gloomy haze of the surrounding trees. He glanced at the clock on the dashboard and was surprised to see it said 5:10PM.

How long have I been sitting here? An hour? Two?

He realised he had no idea. There was a map in the glove compartment, which he spread across his lap and examined. It looked like a bunch of crooked lines in various colours, none of which appeared to be the side road he was on.

From outside the car, another flash of movement caught his notice. He looked up, hoping to glimpse what darted amongst the trees. Besides the drizzle, nothing. *A trick of the water on the windshield. Had to be.*

His mind drifted to thoughts of creatures that didn't take shelter from the rain. Was he better off to hunker down in the car for the night, or try to walk out to safety? And which way to walk if he did? He'd already driven forty or fifty kilometers, too far to walk. On the other hand, how close was he to the other side of his little shortcut? It could be as far, or even more, before he reached pavement again. Given the crushing isolation, neither seemed especially appealing. Plus there was the thing moving around out there, watching him.

He struck the steering wheel with the palm of his hand. *Nothing in the forest is out to get you. Stop it.* Still, the prospect of walking an undetermined distance in a driving rain appealed to him less with each passing minute. He looked at the clock again. 5:46. A few hours of daylight left. The temperature had already dropped noticeably. He decided it made sense to stay put, stay dry, and get through the night.

His stomach rumbled, and it occurred to him that he hadn't eaten anything since breakfast, nearly ten hours earlier. He rummaged through the console between the seats and found half a candy bar. He ate it in one bite and washed it down with a splash of cold coffee from his travel mug. None of it did anything to ease his hunger . He lit another smoke and tried to ignore his discomfort.

By seven it was dark enough that any lingering thoughts of escape were forgotten. The rain hammered steadily on the roof of the car, noisy, but oddly soothing. He adjusted the driver's seat as far back as he could and tried to get comfortable. It frightened him to think that the car might slide the rest of the way into the ditch while he slept. What if he woke up neck-deep in slimy, viscous mud, trapped inside at the mercy of doors that refused to open? He imagined the cold shock, as the sludge from the ditch rose ever higher and continued to swallow up the car. Despite his fear, under the circumstances he'd have to risk it. The only alternative was to try and find a dry place among the trees, which seemed unlikely. With a shiver he pulled his jacket up around him and tried to drift off to sleep. He imagined he could feel the car sinking deeper into the mud.

It's only your imagination, relax.

He awoke with a violent shiver, cold and disoriented. The rain had stopped; the night was pitch black, still and quiet. He rubbed his eyes and tried to figure out what had roused him. He blew on his hands and stuffed them into his pockets for warmth. The dashboard clock read 4:13AM.

Lucas cursed his stupidity. Impatience had placed him in this dangerous predicament in the first place, and things had only gotten worse as the day wore on. His body ached from the cold and cramped confines of the car. He decided to step out and stretch, but his hand froze on the door handle, when he heard an unfamiliar sound. From somewhere in the darkness he could hear a sloshing, sucking noise, like heavy footsteps in thick mud. Steadily, noisily, the footsteps grew louder. Something was out there, and came toward him.

He huddled down in his seat and tried to make himself as small and inconspicuous as possible. He couldn't see anything in the blackness, but that didn't mean something couldn't see him. The footsteps became louder, as they drew nearer, and then stopped suddenly right outside the car. Lucas squeezed his eyes shut and held his breath. He imagined being watched through the window, and he squirmed away from the door.

The car shuddered, as something heavy brushed against it. Lucas clapped his hands over his mouth to stifle a scream. Through the closed windows he heard a deep, rumbling growl. He inched even further down into his seat. A thought occurred to him, and he reached for the door lock. He placed his thumb over it and, with a wince of dread, pressed down. It made the faintest of clicks, barely audible. He exhaled slowly, but his breath caught in his throat and his eyes widened. The other three were probably not activated. He considered pressing the button, but feared the noise would alert the monster to his presence.

Even though he couldn't see the thing, it was large enough to rock the car and could probably come right through the window if it wanted. If that was the case, locked doors wouldn't matter. He did reach across and lock the front passenger door, a token gesture that made him feel slightly better. He peered over the dash from his cramped position and strained for a sign of the beast. For long minutes, he neither heard nor saw any sign of activity, but was unconvinced the threat was over. Gradually, he drifted into a fitful sleep.

He stirred to life at the first rays of dawn. His muscles throbbed, and he grimaced as he stepped out onto the road. The car didn't seem to have moved much in the night, no marks indicated anything had struck it.

Did I dream the whole thing?

It had all seemed far too real for that to be the case. Either way, he was thankful the car hadn't slid the rest of the way into the ditch while he had slept.

The road, spongy and wet, sucked at his shoes, but he barely noticed. He focused his attention entirely on the footprints that surrounded his car near the front and driver's side. They were unlike any tracks he'd ever seen. He placed his foot beside one for perspective. Even washed out by the rain, it was several inches longer than his own foot, and nearly twice as wide. He stared in horrified fascination, as he realised something frighteningly large had passed outside the car in the night. It was possible – probable, even – that it had watched him through the windows while he slept.

He could not spend another night in the woods. He had no idea what sort of creature had left those prints, but he wanted no part of it. Exposed and vulnerable outside the relative safety of the car, he reassured himself that nocturnal prowlers would be asleep by day. Once he'd made up his mind to leave, the only thing left to determine was which direction – go back the way he'd come, or continue toward his destination. It would probably be faster to press onward, since the map indicated he should be somewhere close to the point where the dirt road rejoined the highway. His stomach rumbled, his joints ached, and he'd barely slept. He shivered from the morning chill, then slowly trudged to the center of the road and into the unknown.

It wasn't long before he realised there was no way he'd have made it to the end of the shortcut. The road had deteriorated to a narrow dirt path. It would have been impossible to manoeuvre his car any further. It gave him an odd sense of satisfaction that he would have still had to walk at some point. Notwithstanding, he'd have been forced to turn around and probably would have gotten stuck anyway.

The sun burned off the last of the early morning chill and hinted at a hot and humid day ahead.

I sure could use a drink.

Despite the heat, he kept to the middle of the road, mostly because of the bugs. All along the edges, where the trees and brush leaned in close and puddles of wet mud persisted, clouds of mosquitoes and midges swirled in a thick haze. Plenty of them still managed to find him where he walked, but he assumed they would be much worse among the trees.

At some point, he became aware of the complete stillness that surrounded him on all sides. Once he took notice, he realised he was the only source of noise in the vicinity. He stopped and stood still and listened to the silence. It unnerved him. Trapped out in the open, he felt small, alone, and vulnerable. With a nervous glance over his shoulder, he took two hurried steps toward the comforting cover of the nearby underbrush.

This afforded him his first real glimpse beyond the edge of the road and into the forest. He noted the damp, mossy ground and the scattering of pine needles that blanketed much of the interior area. He considered how much cooler it looked under the dense cover of the trees. He had reached up to push a branch aside and step in when he saw the beast.

He froze in place and gazed through the trees, awestruck. It took a moment to grasp what he witnessed, and he was thankful he'd stopped before it spotted him. Even from a distance, he knew he wanted this creature to overlook him. At first, he thought it might be a big cat, like a panther. The only experience he had with large predators was in a zoo, and the thing before him dwarfed them all. Massive, both in height and bulk, it crept along with a graceful, feline gait. It had a coat of thick, matted black fur, and although Lucas couldn't clearly make out the head, he thought he saw a glimpse of curved horns, like those of a ram. A long, whip-like tail dragged in the dirt behind it.

Lucas stared in fascination and terror. The mystifying presence of such a creature aside, he was struck by the way it moved silently through the woods. Twigs, dried sticks, and rocks littered the ground. Branches hung from every nearby tree, and leafy underbrush filled the gaps between them. Yet, the beast moved with such stealth and somehow managed to avoid every noisy obstacle in its path.

Lucas crouched behind the bushes, frozen in fear, and prayed the hideous beast would pass by unaware of his presence. The creature plodded along at a steady pace and stared straight ahead, as though it were oblivious to its surroundings. It halted and raised its great shaggy head, nostrils twitching, as it sniffed the air.

Oh, shit.

Lucas sucked in a sharp breath, frozen, barely able to blink. His heart thudded and he tried to will it to stop, convinced the creature would hear it and spot him.

The beast swung its shaggy head from side to side, testing the air. Its lupine ears stood erect and alert, and its eyes narrowed, as it scanned the foliage all around. For a moment, the creature's gaze paused on the bushes where Lucas stood.

Certain he'd been discovered—had it looked right at him?—the beast made no indication. With a watery snort, it strode off into the depths of the forest out of sight.

Lucas remained still and quiet, until he could no longer hear the creature's passage through the trees. His hands trembled uncontrollably, and he stuffed them into his pockets. He slumped to a seated position, closed his eyes and drew a deep breath. After several minutes, he heard the distant call of a bird, then the answering cry of another much closer. The low drone of a mosquito made him realise the forest had crept back to life, which meant the danger had passed for the time being. He stood and stretched, glancing around to make sure the creature hadn't paused nearby to silently observe and stalk him.

Confident that the immediate threat had passed, he focused on how to escape the forest. He'd walked for hours and had come far, but now he knew the monster had gone this way, too. If he turned back he'd be forced to spend a second night in the woods. Another encounter with the beast didn't appeal to him, but another night was unthinkable.

That thing's got to be long gone by now, right? This forest is huge, it could be anywhere by now.

Unconvinced, but with no better option, he began to walk once again. Little changed along the path while he walked. Time and distance lost all meaning beyond the prospect of putting one foot in front of the other, over and over again. Though the creature never entirely left his thoughts, the danger became less immediate the further he walked. The trees seemed to blur into a single unbroken entity and his mind drifted to thoughts of other things that lived in the woods. He decided it had been a wise choice to stick to the path, where he could at least see anything dangerous before it was upon him.

As the afternoon sun began its gradual descent and with untold miles behind him, Lucas froze in place and listened. Softly, in the distance, he heard the whoosh of a vehicle, as it sped along a road. The hint of a smile spread across his face. He couldn't tell for sure which direction the sound had come from, but he figured as long as he kept going it would intersect the main road sooner or later. He quickened his pace, his energy and optimism renewed.

The Sound of Passing Traffic

He ran as long as he could then slowed, red-faced and out of breath. He'd heard the sound of a vehicle twice more and felt sure he had to be close, and willed himself forward. At a bend in the trail, he stopped and leaned against a tree for a breather. His hair matted his forehead and his feet ached. He winced at the sting of sweat in his eyes, and dabbed at them with his shirt sleeve. A thick cloud of mosquitoes, drawn to the sweat and the frantic waving of his hands, had tormented him mercilessly in increasing numbers as the day wore on. The growing swarm had pushed him forward, and he had found temporary relief only when he ran for brief stretches. Over the hum of the insects, he heard another vehicle, even closer than before.

There it is again. Louder now. The highway has to be close. Got to keep going.

He pushed away from the tree and trotted onward, with a mental note to veer to the right wherever possible. It crossed his mind to plunge into the woods and proceed cross-country in the direction he wanted, but decided against it. Even as unaccustomed to the woods as he was, he knew how easy it would be to get lost in the forest with no landmarks of any kind, nor any way to keep track of distance or direction. If he got lost in the woods, he would never come out again.

He stopped with a confused frown. Another car passed, this time directly behind him.

How is that possible? Did I move in a circle somehow?

Ahead, at the furthest reaches of his vision, he saw what looked like a clearing in the otherwise unbroken forest. He questioned whether to go back and get his bearings or go ahead and explore the new anomaly in the landscape. The shadows had grown longer, as the day wore on. He couldn't waste time to backtrack. On top of that, he'd started to feel queasy and light-headed.

Still, he'd been chasing a sound for what felt like hours. It had kept him on the move past the point of exhaustion, beyond the faint sliver of faint hope he'd clung to all day. With great reluctance, he returned to the bend in the trail. It veered back around to the right, as gradually as he remembered. He spotted the tree he'd leaned against earlier. As he approached, he slowed to a walk. He gaped, wide-eyed, at the four deep gashes that scarred the trunk at shoulder height.

He stopped a few feet away, raised his hand to his mouth, and stared. The marks ran parallel to one another, about two inches apart. They had shredded the thick bark like paper and cut deeply into the tree.

Did I not notice them before? I'm exhausted, and the bugs are driving me crazy. Could I have missed this somehow?

He tried to convince himself the marks were old, but in his heart it seemed unlikely. These were fresh.

He traced his fingers along one of the scratches and noted their deepness. They were some sort of claw marks, though he had no idea what could have left them. Other than a large bear, he couldn't imagine anything else powerful enough to have done such a thing.

You know what did this, and it wasn't a bear.

There was something that could – he'd seen it in the woods earlier. He couldn't recall whether it had claws or not, but anything that large and sinister almost certainly did.

A wave of desperation gripped him. He was lost and alone, at great risk of sickness or hypothermia, and unable to locate the highway. A monster with huge claws lurked nearby. His second day in the forest neared its end, and the shadows seemed to grow longer than they had before.

While he stood there and pondered, afternoon shifted towards early evening. He'd spent most of his time and energy trying to locate the traffic's direction. Now, darkness cloaked the road. One portion of shadow—too long and out of place, even for the lateness of the day—separated from the greater blackness and swayed back and forth like a pendulum.

Or a cat's tail before it pounces.

Lucas felt his body go rigid with fear. With shoulders hunched, he slowly turned around. In the middle of the road, fewer than ten paces away, stood the beast.

As badly as the creature had frightened him the first time, from a relatively safe distance, it was even more terrifying. It towered over Lucas, and peered down at him from a height well above his own. Its face split into a toothy grin, and its eyes gleamed with anticipation. Lucas noted with dismay that the beast did indeed have claws—long, wickedly curved ones whose tips dug into the crusty mud of the path.

It slowly lowered itself into a crouch, its hindquarters up, like a tightly coiled spring. The long tail no longer dragged on the ground, but stood upright, and the tip twitched back and forth. Lucas stared in amazement at the creature's tail, which made a hollow swoosh, as it moved. It sounded exactly like a car passing on a distant highway. He realised with dismay there was no road, and there were no cars. The creature had been stalking him the entire time.

With its ears laid flat against its head, the creature curled its lips in a ferocious sneer and gave a tremendous roar. Lucas winced and he dropped to his knees, covering his ears. He felt the ground tremble, as the creature charged, and he closed his eyes.

Biographies

COLLEEN ANDERSON is a Canadian author who has been twice nominated for the *Aurora Award* in poetry, several times for a Rhysling award, and longlisted for the *Stoker Award* in fiction. As a freelance editor, she has co-edited *Tesseracts 17* and Aurora nominated for *Playground of Lost Toys*. *Alice Unbound: Beyond Wonderland (2018 - Exile Publishing)* is her first solo anthology. She has served on both *Stoker Award* and *British Fantasy Award* juries, and guest edited *Eye to the Telescope*. Over 200 works have seen print with some recent pieces in *Polu Texni*, *The Future Fire*, *Thrilling Words*, *Beauty of Death*, and many others. Her fiction collection, *A Body of Work* was recently published by *Black Shuck Books, UK*. She is also working on a poetry collection and alternate world novel.
www.colleenanderson.wordpress.com

JUDITH BARON is a speculative fiction writer. Her work has been published in Animal Uprising, Future Visions Anthologies: Volume 2, Horror Bites Magazine Issue #8, The Poet's Haven Digest: It Was a Dark and Stormy Night, Deadly Bargain: A Colors in Darkness Anthology, Spadina Literary Review and Trembling with Fear. She has a Bachelor of Arts degree in

English from the University of Western Ontario, and currently lives near Toronto, Ontario with her husband and child.

KAREN DALES is the award winning author of the Amazon best selling series, *The Chosen Chronicles,* which include *Changeling, Angel of Death, Shadow of Death*, and *Thanatos.* Her short fiction works have been published in various international anthologies. She has been an author guest at such conventions as Fan Expo Toronto, Anime North, Polaris and many others. She is also the managing editor for Dark Dragon Publishing and teaches Creative Writing for the City of Toronto. www.karendales.com

PAT FLEWWELLINGING is a multi-genre author and the owner of **Myth Hawker Travelling Bookstore**. In her spare time, she's also a part-time freelance editor and a full-time senior business analyst in telecommunications. The fourth installment of her science fiction/horror series, *Helix Sedition*, is due out mid-August, 2019.

JEN FRANKEL is the author of the Blood & Magic series as well as the vegan zombie romantic comedy, *Undead Redhead.* Her work has appeared in various anthologies and magazines including Amazing Stories.

Award Winning Author, TYNER GILLIES, is a storyteller, lawman, Scotch drinker, and a bit of a meat head. His novels— *The Watch, Dark Resolution, The Black Door,* and *Shadowboxing*— centre around his hometown. He lives and works in the Fraser Valley, BC with his wife and a cat who is mostly a pain in the ass. www.tynergillies.com

A life-long lover of horror, VANESSA C. HAWKINS wrote her first story in the genre when she was only in grade five. It was titled Mutilated and it warranted her a trip to the school guidance counselor. A lifetime later, she continues to write about anything gruesome, terrifying, paranormal and erotic, though she has since found herself enthralled in the lighthearted world of fantasy steampunk. Her first two books *Gloryhill* and *A Sinister Portrait of Cherie Rose* exemplify her fascination with the weird. Her work has been featured in anthologies in South Korea and the US. Just recently, she published a steampunk fantasy novel entitled *The Curious Case of Simon Todd* through Books We Love Publishing.

REPO KEMPT has spent over fifteen years working as a criminal lawyer in the remote communities of the Canadian Arctic. He is a regular columnist for Litreactor.com and a member of the Horror Writers Association. He currently lives in Nova Scotia.

NANCY KILPATRICK is an award-winning author. Her publishing credits include 22 novels, over 220 short stories, 6 collections of her stories, 1 graphic novel, 1 non-fiction book and, as well, she has edited 15 anthologies. She lives in Montreal and her work is published in the U.S., Canada, the U.K., with translations into 8 languages. These are the genres in which she has published: dark fantasy, horror, fantasy, mystery, science fiction, erotica. Her most recent works are 4 of 6 vampire novels in the series *Thrones of Blood*, Details can be found on her website: nancykilpatrick.com

CAITLIN MARCEAU is an author and professional editor living and working in Montreal, Quebec. She holds a B.A. in Creative Writing, is a member of both the Horror Writers Association and the Quebec Writers' Federation, and spends most of her time writing horror and experimental fiction.

She's been published for journalism, poetry, as well as creative non-fiction, and has spoken about horror literature at several Canadian conventions. Her workshop "Bikinis, Brains, and Boogeymen: How To Write Realistic Women In Horror," was acclaimed by Yell Magazine, and her first co-authored collection, Read-Only: A Collection of Digital Horror was released in June of 2017.

As of 2018, she is the co-owner and CEO of Sanitarium, an indie publishing house dedicated to encouraging diverse voices in horror media.

If she's not covered in ink or wading through stacks of paper, you can find her ranting about issues in pop culture or nerding out over a good book. For more information, or just to say hi, you can reach her through infocaitlinmarceau@gmail.com

JOE POWERS is a Canadian horror writer and long-time fan of all things scary. From his introduction to the genre on a stormy Saturday night at the age of six—his first viewing of Bride of Frankenstein—he's been hooked. Among his many inspirations, he lists Stephen King, Jack Ketchum, Michael Crichton, Vincent Price and Richard Matheson. He enjoys introducing the reader to flawed, believable characters, and leading them on dark journeys with an unexpected twist. His work has appeared in various anthologies and collections, and his debut novel is scheduled to release in 2019. In his spare time he's an avid hockey fan and creative writing instructor. He lives in New Brunswick with his wife, Sheryl, and an assortment of furry creatures. Follow Joe at www.joepowersauthor.com.

ROBIN ROWLAND is a writer and photographer based in Kitimat, BC, best known for co-writing the first popular computer manual on how to search the internet published in 1995. He is co-author of nonfiction biographies of Canadian Prohibition gangster Rocco Perri and RCMP undercover ace Frank Zaneth and author of A River Kwai Story about the POWs on the Burma Thailand Railway. He has contributed short stories to the Darkover anthologies and is currently working on a climate change based fantasy novel. For most of his career his day job was working as writer, lineup editor, producer and photographer for CBC News.

DAVID TOCHER lives and works in Kelowna, BC. He writes fiction that explores the paranormal and the dark side of human nature.

SARA C. WALKER is a Canadian author who writes urban fantasy novels, speculative short fiction, and poetry. She has never hunted a living creature, but does enjoy hiking through forests. Sara lives and writes next to a lake in the beautiful cottage country of Central Ontario. You can find out more at www.sarawalker.ca.

54975026R00120

Made in the USA
Middletown, DE
17 July 2019